Burnt Out

BURNT OUT

Susan Koefod

NORMANDALE COMMUNITY COLLEGE
LIBRARY
9700 FRANCE AVENUE SOUTH
BLOOMINGTON, MN 55431-4399

NORTH STAR PRESS OF ST. CLOUD, INC.
Saint Cloud, Minnesota

Copyright © 2013 Susan Koefod

ISBN 978-0-87839-663-4

All rights reserved.

This is a work of fiction. Names, characters, places, and incidents are the products of the author's imagination or are used fictitiously. Any resemblance to actual events or persons, living or dead, is entirely coincidental.

First Edition: September 2013

Printed in the United States of America

Published by
North Star Press of St. Cloud, Inc.
P.O. Box 451
St. Cloud, Minnesota 56302

www.northstarpress.com   "Like" us on Facebook!

Dedication

For Ryan, who loves language and teaches me everyday about how to be unafraid of being who you are.

1

CHRISTINE IVORY KNEW SHE had been spotted the moment she exited the highway. Lucid, Minnesota, was like that. Eyes were always everywhere, keeping watch, quickly determining whether friends or enemies were entering the territory, ready to welcome the former and shun the latter. She was pretty sure which camp she'd fall into. She wasn't a native like her deceased father, Rob Ivory, had been. And she wasn't his cute little girl anymore either. She'd been an exile for years and was sure she wouldn't be welcomed back.

And if she made the wrong choice about what to do with her father's expansive property, the town's opinion of her would only worsen. The scrutiny hit her full force as she passed by an enormous billboard just off the interstate. The face of a local realtor—a familiar face she couldn't place—practically leered at her as she passed by. She didn't note the name, not wanting to hold the billboard realtor's eyes longer than necessary. She got the feeling the face on the sign was demanding an explanation from her. What made her think she belonged in Lucid?

But she'd had lots of critics over the years. She'd gotten used to people hating her guts. One person, in particular, came to mind. Detective Arvo Thorson, her former co-worker, her former lover, her permanent nemesis. But she was several hundred miles away from him now. She was going to put him behind her, at last. Besides, memories of another significant man in her life were rushing in, filling in the gaps.

There simply wasn't any space left for Arvo in her life.

That was what she willed herself to believe, as a vision of the slouchy, stained, middle-aged detective flashed in her mind. The last time she'd seen him, he was recovering from serious injuries after solving a case they'd worked on together. The sight of him in that hospital bed reminded her how close she had been to losing him, for good. That same day she'd met his new love, an artist named Jade.

"She seems really smart. And nice," Christine had said.

"She is," Arvo said, quickly adding, "You're smart, too, Christine."

"But not very nice?"

"I left that part out as a joke."

"We both know it's no joke." She sighed and held out her hand. "So it's goodbye?"

"Why so hesitant in your farewells?" he said, his voice stronger. "Given how things have gone with us, you should be celebrating that you're finally going to be free of me. So say it like you mean it, Christine. I want a goddamned goodbye."

She gave him his "goddamed goodbye," both of them holding back tears. It was really over, and Christine thought she was ready, at last, to move on.

So as she drove up the black-walnut-lined driveway of her father's property in late spring, instead of mulling over Arvo's shortcomings, the sad end of their relationship, and the last difficult months of work in Somerset County, she thought about what her father had taught her, years before. His repeated lessons were all about how geological history lay hidden in the landscape. She thought this topic, which had bored her as a girl, would at least distract her from her recent past, and set the tone for the tedious work that lay ahead.

The memories quickly flooded to the surface from where they had lain, undisturbed, in the decade since the man died, and in the many years since she'd been the little girl at his side.

Her dad had told her more than once how the land's belly was full of glacial till. How its bald hilltops, its fish-filled lakes, its thickly wooded and game-filled depressions, and its nearly treeless savannahs had been scoured and shaped by advancing and retreating glaciers. He'd taken her to places where he could point out the crested contours of the last glacier's final stand, still visible even though the melt-water lake left by the retreating ice—larger than the five Great Lakes—had dried up eons ago. When the glacial Lake Agassiz finally drained away, taking with it a good deal of the landscape, it left behind a huge, wasted beach that covered thousands of miles and a flat, depressed tract (the ancient lake bottom) that to this day flooded as easily as an elderly spinster's eyes.

As she advanced down his rutted driveway, she reflected on the many times she'd given her father a sullen face when he told her all about the glaciers. Why was it now, when he was long gone, that her grief was emerging anew?

She knew what her father would have told her. His story was consistent, and for a corporate guy who saved every penny, invested in land in the town where he was raised, and retired early to live out his life where he was born, he was absolutely passionate about it.

"Don't give me that face, Chrissy. Pay attention. I don't care if you think this is boring or you think it doesn't matter. It does."

They had been standing together on the hilltop above his property. She, a bored sixteen-year-old, and Rob Ivory not yet fifty. He had nearly finished assembling the fine spread of prime landscape just outside of Lucid and had just finished building a snug two-bedroom cabin on it.

He turned professorial, and adopted a serious tone. "We're formed from our environment, Chrissy, tuned into it. It affects us in more ways than we can possibly know."

She grimaced.

"Okay, maybe that's a bit of a stretch." He laughed.

"You've told me this stuff a million times before, Daddy," she said, kicking a clod of dirt in the field. She wanted to cry out and run away. She couldn't bear to hear his dry, boring geology lecture again. Why couldn't she be back inside, organizing his receipts for his recently purchased tools, putting away the second-hand dishes she'd found in a second-hand store in Pelican Rapids, sweeping and tidying the small kitchen.

"Humor me. Pretend there's a lesson in all of this," he said. He gave her a long look. "You'll come up with something."

Even then, as a bratty teen, she knew he just wanted for her to share his love for the landscape, his enthusiasm for—ahem—rocks.

She sighed and stopped twitching. Maybe if she paid attention a bit longer, he'd finish the lecture and they could go inside. Thoughts of the pretty yellow floral plates she'd found focused her. She'd give them a good scrub in hot soapy water and then they'd really shine.

"Just look how those glacier-scarred boulders unexpectedly surface in a farm field," he said, pointing some distance away where some boulders had emerged on a hilltop. "One day they are below the surface, the next day they come up and tear your tractor apart."

His eyes brightened and he gave her a wink. "Here's the lesson from the old man, courtesy of the glaciers. You can only push stuff down for so long. It WILL come back to tear you to pieces."

"Right, daddio," she'd said, flippantly.

HE HAD BEEN RIGHT, SHE THOUGHT SADLY. More than he even knew.

The gravel pinged beneath her tires and ricocheted off her Jetta's underbody, and her mourning overwhelmed her. It was many times more visceral than what she'd experienced at his funeral, though to be honest the shock of his unexpected death had probably numbed her.

Now the pain left her gasping.

She shouldn't have been surprised by how hidden grief can sometimes resurface, years later. Her training told her it wasn't entirely unexpected. Still, she never applied her expert level social worker skills, gained from years of experience working with her fragile, young patients, to herself. She was a grown woman, in the middle of middle age, toughened by years of work with crime victims and witnesses. Everyone knew, including Christine, that she rarely cried. Yet here she was, not more than five minutes inside Lucid town limits, and she felt like she'd be weeping for many days to come.

She stopped midway along the driveway and waited for her sobs to subside. When she finally calmed down, she got out of her car, knowing she needed to take in the whole scene before she could begin the long-put-off task that brought her to Lucid. The gravel driveway's unevenness was amplified by the litter of lime-sized black walnut fruits, some of which had been chewed open by squirrels or run over by the farm vehicles working her father's fields. As sure-footed as she normally was in her high-heeled boots, for the weeks of manual labor ahead she'd need the work boots she knew were inside the cabin, ones she'd worn as a teenager when she'd traipsed the countryside so many summers ago.

She knew that once the decade anniversary hit she could no longer make the excuses she'd been making. It had officially been too long. Her mother had been on her for years to either put the place up for sale or take a more active interest in managing it. She'd been the lone owner since her father's death, but she had remained an absentee landlord. Her father's lifelong friend, and Lucid's only cop, Ted Nelson, had managed everything for her. It was too much for Ted to manage, now that he was getting on in years, though he never complained.

She'd thought she had good reasons for putting off the trip to Lucid: her social worker caseload in Mendota County never let up. She'd been the lead social worker in the Mendota County Social Services department, and handled the toughest cases. But it took its toll, and even though she'd lasted longer than most, tough-as-nails Christine Ivory eventually got to the breaking point. People were shocked to learn she'd turned in her notice, but she knew a fair many who were glad to see her go.

She wasn't exactly sure where Arvo stood, but that didn't matter any more. And now that she'd quit her job, there were no more excuses. She had another offer for the same job in another county, and she'd set a start date for the coming fall, giving herself a badly needed break. She'd driven up from the Twin Cities that morning, after cleaning out her condo's refrigerator, dropping by her mother's place with the few groceries she had, and leaving a forwarding address at the post office.

She looked across the wide expanse of land her father had acquired, quarter section by quarter section, over the years. He'd kept a small, nearly empty apartment in Minneapolis—not more than a place to drop his suitcases and store his business clothes—and spent every weekend and every vacation in Lucid, his hometown. He and Christine's mother had been divorced longer then she remembered them being married, so like her father, Christine considered the Lucid property her father's place, rarely, if ever, setting foot in his city apartment.

Movement flickered in the trees, which were already leafy and summer dark green, unlike the just planted, muddy fields that surrounded her. She wasn't surprised to hear a vehicle turn off the county road and begin to drive up the long driveway. She knew who it would be. She quickly dabbed away the remains of her tears, thankful that her waterproof mascara would leave no telltale stains down her cheeks. She blew her nose hastily and tossed the used tissue with the rest of the pile that had accumulated on the passenger seat.

"Hey, Christine!" the familiar voice called out. It was Ted. As the town's only cop, even if he hadn't been the one who first spotted her, word would have made its way quickly to him. She wondered how he could have found time to be away from his duty patrolling Lucid, considering it was a Saturday afternoon, and that was a popular time of the day to catch up with the citizenry of Lucid on their way through town for groceries, barbering, swapping fish stories, refilling boat fuel, or just generally shooting the breeze at the town's only restaurant.

But he wasn't in his squad car, the only one the Lucid Police Department possessed. Instead, he got out of a rusty Chevy pickup wearing civilian clothes. She'd never seen the pickup before, and given the amount of rust on it, he'd had it for some time. The last car, in fact the only car she'd ever seen him in was the squad. He'd led the funeral procession from the Lutheran church to the cemetery, spoken at her father's funeral, and arranged the twenty-one-gun salute for his fellow Korean War veteran.

He approached her, offering up a bear hug, which she accepted warily, wondering how much of it was for her, how much for his deceased and treasured friend.

"Still all skin and bones," he said. "I didn't hear from your mom you were coming." Neither of her parents had remarried after their divorce, yet her mother remained connected to goings on in Lucid.

"Well, she didn't know," Christine admitted quickly, without any feeling of guilt. She'd given her mother little in the way of explanation. She hadn't even told her mother she'd quit her job. Dorla Ivory didn't need any ammunition for a gossipy call to Lucid, or even a chat with her friends at the Tin Cup, the little restaurant directly below her apartment in St. Paul. Christine wasn't entirely sure how she herself felt about her job, her future, her immediate plans in Lucid. She wasn't going to work them out in a blowout discussion with her mother, then have her words chewed on by

Dorla and her friend Margie during their daily afternoon gossip at the Tin Cup.

"You could have called, you know that, Chrissy," Ted said.

Chrissy. Only her father and his closest friends in Lucid called her that. She'd considered going by the name during her college years, but didn't. It felt too little girlish. Still, her given name, Christine, always felt wrong to her, even though it was the way her mother and almost everyone else referred to her.

Chrissy was the name reserved for people who really knew her, the secret key to her soul, her past, the real person she was that she kept bottled up inside. It sounded normal coming from Ted, but it had been years since she'd regularly seen him, so it troubled her at first to hear the name. Used by the wrong person at the wrong time, the name almost felt insulting. Condescending. The kind of thing you'd call a woman to make her feel like a little girl who couldn't take care of herself. And who didn't admit she really wanted or needed to be taken care of. Sometimes.

"I'd have come and opened up the place for you," he said, "gotten things ready, had Ruth come over and clean the place up a bit."

Ted looked more hurt than angry. She told herself to back off. He wasn't an enemy, trying to make her feel like she couldn't take care of herself. He was practically family. "I'm sorry, Ted. That's why I didn't call. I didn't want to bother you." *I can handle it*, she thought. *I don't want people asking me or prying until I'm ready. Even family.* Her mother and Margie, gossiping over cigarettes, came to mind. *Especially family.*

"Well, you know it wouldn't have bothered me at all. Not one bit," he said, putting an arm around her as they both looked towards the house. "I'd drop everything to help Robbie's little girl."

"I know. I'm sorry." Christine let him hold her. He was the same age as her dad, and now that ten years had passed, Ted had to be closing in on seventy. He looked eerily similar to her dad. Maybe that was how it was with the older generation of Lucid.

Somewhere along the way, almost everyone was related. She recalled that Ted's mother and her grandmother had been second or third cousins. She might have been looking at a version of her dad, at least what he might have become had he lived another ten years. Ted had a stiff thatch of white-gray hair. His skin was already deeply tanned, the sun-baked lines permanently chiseled into his face, a given for a man who'd spent most of his life outdoors, many of them in fishing boats over the years.

"So what's with the civilian clothes? On a Saturday afternoon? I'm not sure I've ever seen you in blue jeans. Ever," she said.

"I retired this past spring. You didn't hear that did you, from your mom? I'm sure I told her."

"You probably did," she said. "My job kept me pretty busy this past year, so there wasn't much time to catch up on Lucid."

"Yes, of course. How are things in Mendota County?" He asked.

She told him they were fine, not ready to give him a significant detail about Mendota County yet. That she was no longer employed there.

"You heard from your mom, didn't you, that someone had rented the place last year?" Ted asked.

"No," Christine said, "I didn't. But I'm sure it was fine. I know you've been looking after the place since Dad died. We've always completely trusted your judgment, especially since we knew that the law was on our side. Getting some rental income to help pay for upkeep, always a good idea."

"I hated to see the place sit there empty, you know, after your dad was gone." Even Ted hadn't quite finished grieving over the loss of his best friend. He cleared his throat. "Plus, if I have someone in there I can trust, I don't have to worry about kids getting up there and running wild."

The guy still had a cop's instinct. Empty houses were an open advertisement for vandalism. Lucid, like any other place, had its share of abandoned houses, given the economy. She was pretty sure Ted had been called in when a house was being repossessed, and had the unpleasant duty of telling friends and possibly relatives that their property was being turned over to a bank, that they had to leave a place they'd considered home. Having someone he trusted looking after his old buddy's place meant he had one less headache.

"How long was he here?" she asked. "The renter."

"Well, that's just it. He planned to leave, right before Christmas."

"Planned to? So, is he still there? Still renting?" She wondered if perhaps she should have called after all. She'd been stupid to think the place might be empty.

"Well, see that's the thing. No one exactly knows where he went after he left."

"Wait. No one knows where he is?" Not even the town's lone cop at the time knew when the guy left? And where he was now? What exactly was she stepping into?

Christine grabbed her purse from the car. "But he's gone, right?"

"As far as we know. But we're not sure where he is. And that's the thing."

"You keep saying, *that's the thing*, then you never quite get to 'the thing.'" Christine knew this sounded like another one of Ted's long, wandering, but usually interesting stories. Much patience was required in talking to Ted, as there were numerous meanders off into what seemed like insignificant, not terribly relevant detail, but somehow, all the pieces came together in the end. You were generally rewarded with a laugh, or shocked with the outcome, sometimes both. His ability to keep track of all the details undoubtedly helped in his police work.

In moments like this, it seemed like she'd never been away for as long as she had. They were right back in the comfortable relationship they'd always had, one of the few comfortable relationships she had with a man in her life. Probably the only one. For him, *Chrissy* was acceptable.

"Come on, let's just leave the cars here and walk the rest of the way in. You can tell me more about this renter *thing* while we walk. I feel the need to make a slow entrance, not sure why. I just don't feel in any particular hurry to get in there. As long as I'm not keeping you from something? What with it being a Saturday afternoon in the prime of fishing season?"

"The fish bite early, I've already been out, got my limit of bluegills, and come in for the afternoon. I have plenty of time to catch up with Robby's girl."

Christine began to walk ahead, then turned to catch him looking at her.

"I'll tell you those boots of yours are going to get you attention you probably don't want around here," he said.

She looked at him and smiled. She had long ignored what people thought of her wardrobe.

"Well not that the rest of the outfit is in keeping with the usual around here," he added.

Christine was wearing something she thought casual, a find at her favorite consignment shop in the city: Bobby Wick's Do-Over. It was a tight, retro late 1960s floral frock Bobby had set aside the moment he saw it, knowing it was perfect for Christine. He'd been right, but of course the look was all wrong in Lucid, she knew.

"You look like Goldie Hawn from her Laugh-in days," Ted said. "No one wore that stuff around here back in the '60s. Looks great on you, of course. I'm just saying. Not sure the farmers' wives and Lucid schoolteachers will appreciate that much. They'll think you're trying to show off and make them look bad."

"I know," she said. "I usually don't care if I raise some eyebrows." She'd been known for her killer wardrobe back in Mendota County. Few people knew that she bought her designer wardrobe second-hand at Bobby Wick's, and given the economy, there was a lot to chose from as the former social climbers who crashed to earth when the financial markets melted down were scrambling to sell off anything of value, and fast. Bobby even had to turn away sellers. He had enough stock to comfortably fill his racks for years, so now he took only the best, and saved the best of the best for Christine.

"I'm pretty sure there are some more Lucid-appropriate clothes in there," she said. Her figure hadn't changed much since her college days, and she knew there were two or three pairs of blue jeans and a fair number of plain cotton shirts that could quickly tone down the wardrobe.

She took Ted's arm, knowing it would make him feel needed and helpful to escort her to the house. She rarely made that accommodation to men, insisting on making her own way over whatever treacherous ground she might encounter. But Ted was family. In some ways, better than family, she thought, reflecting on her mother.

"So, what's this thing about the renter? Hopefully he was all paid up," she said with a wink.

"He paid ahead. In full. I met the guy, of course. He came in regularly for a bite to eat at the Y Not. In fact, we had dinner there on several occasions. I came out and sat with him in the evenings, what with me being his landlord, of sorts. Your dad would've liked him. I knew it the moment I laid eyes on him."

"It sounded like you liked him."

"Hell, yes," he said.

They strolled along the road, Christine feeling more comfortable then she'd felt in days. Maybe it was being away from the majority of her problems that would help her finally work through the loss of her dad. The lump in her throat slowly melted.

"He was from West Virginia. Said there was plenty of good fishing back there. We talked about getting him out in a boat around here, but he was always too busy with his crew, his research."

"Research?"

"He was studying the rocks around here. Had a huge crew of people with him, though they were staying up in Pelican Falls at the Holiday Inn. He insisted on staying here the whole time. He was some sort of important, famous geologist. Had all sorts of fancy degrees. Everyone on his crew called him Dr. Adams, but we were on a first-name basis from the start."

"A geologist. What on earth would a geologist find of interest around here?"

"You haven't heard about this? I would've thought it'd make it into the Minneapolis papers."

"Well, I don't always get time to read the papers. Actually, I read everything online these days. I don't think I've subscribed for years. In my line of work, we have a pretty low opinion of reporters. Whenever we do make the paper, the story is usually wrong."

"You mean about some criminal case you're involved in?"

Christine nodded.

"Yeah. I had the same problem. You can't always reveal everything to the press, especially when you're dealing with the small town press and the editor's wife's your barber's wife's best friend."

Christine laughed. She knew exactly what he was talking about.

"Ongoing investigations mean you can't say a word at all," he said. "I tell you, it's even tougher when you're the town's only cop and you're related to or friends with almost everyone, too."

"Oh, I know what you're talking about. Somerset Hills isn't quite as small as Lucid, given that it's practically a suburb of Minneapolis, but we had our share of run-ins with the press," she said.

"I tell you, Chrissy. Your dad would tell us about some of the cases you got involved in. I don't know how you did it. Some of those victims you worked with? The terrible things people do, sometimes to their own kids! Unbelievable," he said. "Things don't get quite as bad around here, but we've had our share of sad cases."

Even small towns weren't immune from big city problems. She knew that.

"Your dad told me he never thought you would have the stomach for that kind of thing. Shoot, it used to make you dizzy to be around when your dad and I were cleaning fish," he said.

"You'd make the most of my fears, as I recall," she said, remembering how the two of them would hold a gutted fish in front of her eyes.

Ted chuckled. "Well, boys will be boys. We couldn't help ourselves. Guys love slime, girls don't. Sorry, Chrissy."

Before they knew it, they were standing at the front door. Her grip on Ted's arm tightened. She knew Ted knew she hadn't been inside since her dad died.

"So what happened to the guy?" she said, letting go of his arm and continuing the conversation in order to keep thoughts of her father at bay. "The geologist you liked. The one who didn't exactly leave, but is no longer here? You didn't tell me yet what he was looking for, in the rocks."

"Oh, right. Believe it or not—oil. The guy was looking for oil."

"Oil? In Lucid?"

"Shale oil. Even people who don't subscribe to the newspaper read about shale oil online, right, Chrissy?"

She made a face at him. "Yes, Ted. Even people like me have heard about shale oil. That's the kind that requires fracking, right?" She wanted to show him she wasn't completely out of touch.

Christine had heard that oil company geologists had been studying Western Minnesota for years, convinced that the rumors of a huge shale oil deposit were true, and more importantly, that the oil was the type that could be brought to the surface. It was one thing to discover subterranean oil deposits, and quite another to successfully recover the oil without going broke. Beyond the production costs, there were serious environmental risks: contaminated groundwater, surface spills, and the many health hazards that could result from both.

"I know. It is unbelievable to think there might be oil here in Lucid," he said, surveying the property with a sweep of his eyes. "Right under our feet!"

"Yes. I guess I hadn't heard that people thought oil was here. In Lucid, I mean."

"The guy told me a bit about his research," Ted said. "Your dad, of course, would have been fascinated," he said.

"Oh, I know. He could go on and on about the glaciers," she said. "He would've loved every bit of it, probably offered to help with the analysis."

"Of course when they made that big discovery at the Bakken, and started to bring the oil up, it got even crazier around here."

The Bakken Formation was found in neighboring North Dakota. Located in a 350-million-year-old underground layer of rock was an estimated 3.0 to 4.3 billion barrels of technically recoverable oil. Once the drilling techniques advanced enough to make recovery profitable, the value of the land around the Bakken skyrocketed, and along with it everything else in the vicinity.

"People are making huge amounts of money out there, from the realtors selling trailer homes to the oil workers, to the barbers who cut their hair, to the oil barons," Ted said. "It's really something. Adams told me the area around Lucid *seemed* to be an ideal place for shale oil deposits to be found, though he was pretty skeptical."

Christine learned that Adams and his team had spent the previous summer taking core samples not only in and around Lucid, but as far away as the South and North Dakota borders, and nearly to the Canadian border. He'd exhausted his team with endless sampling requests, overwhelmed every county authority with his unending permit requests, and sent truckloads of material to various labs around the country with very specific, detailed requirements for his analysis.

"Then, after he'd sent his crew back to West Virginia, he decided to spend the winter holed up here, poring over the data. He could have completed this part of the project at home in West Virginia, but he liked the solitude of Lucid, and with the rest of his team gone, he had the peace and quiet he needed."

"Well, did he find any? Oil that is?"

"Well, that's the thing," Ted said without looking at her.

She didn't demand he explain *the thing*. She just waited.

"No one knows," he said.

"No one?" Christine distracted herself, still half-listening to the story while she dug through her purse for her keys.

"I saw him the day he planned to leave. He'd just gotten a haircut, a shave. Said he had just wrapped up his report, but wanted to read through it one more time. Of course, I didn't ask him straight out whether he found anything. He said he couldn't tell anyone anything officially and that made sense to me, you know, given my occupation."

Christine located her keys, but didn't move. Ted was finally getting to the point of his story. She didn't want to distract him.

"Anyway, after he had his shave, he said he was going to get a bottle of bourbon, but didn't know if he had time to run up to Pelican Falls since, of course, the liquor store we had here in Lucid was closed. I told him I had an unopened bottle of Jim Beam, happy to make it a farewell gift to him. We'd shared more than a few nightcaps right here," he said, pointing to her patio. "So I gave him the bottle and that was it."

"That was it?" Christine felt her keys, quickly identifying the one to the house, its textured cap as familiar to her as the callused hand of her dad.

"No one saw him after that. And he never made it back to West Virginia. He just disappeared."

Christine slid the key into the lock, and opened the door to the cabin. "It's sticking," she said, and Ted offered an arm. When they finally managed to get it open, and got inside, they saw that while Dr. Adams had managed to finish packing and remove most of his things, a few random belongings seemed forgotten as he departed.

And apparently undisturbed in the months he'd been missing.

His thick parka. And an unopened bottle of Jim Beam. The same one that he had been given from none other than Lucid's only police officer at the time, now retired, the man who was now standing next to her, scratching his head: her father's lifelong best friend, Ted Nelson.

2

"SINCE YOU DIDN'T TELL ME YET, I HAVE TO ASK. Wasn't there an investigation of Adams' disappearance? Or has this Jim Beam bottle been sitting here, untouched, for six months?" Christine laid her purse on the table, and began to perspire in the stuffy air of the long-closed house.

With the fingerprints of the town cop all over it. Crap, Christine thought. She was sure she was getting away from crime scenes, investigations, witnesses, and anything having to do with her life in Mendota County. She had traveled several hours and two hundred miles to get away from it. Had she not gone far enough away?

"Of course. What do you take us for? The guy's disappearance was investigated." Ted's face reddened.

How much of an investigation was actually done out here? She wanted to ask. But she knew it would have been the most insulting thing she could say, particularly to the guy who was responsible at the time for the investigation. For a moment she considered calling the Carlson County sheriff's department, since maybe it would have been them taking the lead, given Ted's connection to the missing man. But six months had come and gone and there was no sign of an important missing geologist? And his belongings were still sitting in her house? Who knew, the place might be considered a crime scene? *With Ted's fingerprints possibly everywhere.*

"Now, Chrissy. You know that things might be handled a little differently out here than what you're used to in the city. But you can bet that if something needed to be checked out, it's been checked out." Ted looked like he had said all he wanted to say about the incident.

The air had turned from relaxed to tense. She felt her heart beating too fast, her face going too hot. A stranger had been in her dad's house. Now he was missing, possibly dead. And no one had thought to pick up the phone and mention anything to her.

"So, why's his stuff still here in my dad's . . . I mean *my* house, six months later?"

"Chrissy. You need to calm down."

That wasn't what she wanted to hear. Some man telling her what to do. Particularly a man in law enforcement. It brought back uncomfortable, explosive memories she'd prefer to forget. Still, she almost went off on him—she was good and ready to scream at her father's lifelong friend, *Don't tell me to calm down!* But the look on Ted's face—shock on the very image of her father's face—shut her down. Why was she getting involved in business she didn't need to be involved in, anyway? She didn't even know the guy who had disappeared.

"No," she said out loud what she'd been thinking to herself. "Never mind. I don't want to know." She got to work opening all of the windows in the house, and the cool, late-spring air blew inside, stirring long still draperies, blowing dust bunnies out from where they'd gathered the past six months.

"Good girl, Chrissy. It's really not your business. Nor mine anymore. I'm done with police work." He put his hand on her shoulder and while *Christine* might have felt burdened and—frankly—condescended by such a move, *Chrissy* got the message that was intended. It was a caring hand on her shoulder. Full of concern for her welfare.

"I'm sorry, Ted," she said, then shook her head. "I've hardly been here for an hour, and I've already apologized to you. Twice."

She put her hand on top of his. "Can you tell I've needed to take a break from everything?"

"I wasn't going to say that," he said, "but it was kind of obvious."

She'd practically been screaming in Ted's face. Something that would have been completely out of character in her dad's side of the family. Nobody screamed. "Maybe I waited too long."

"You did kind of snap, pretty fast," he took both her hands. "Tell you what. Why don't I go and drive your car up, help you get your things inside. You staying here for a while?"

"Yes, a couple of weeks, at the very least."

"Good. While I'm getting your things inside, why don't you re-familiarize yourself with the place, get things more opened up?"

She nodded. "That sounds like a good idea."

"I'd take a little shot of that bourbon," he said, nodding towards the Jim Beam, "if you'd pour some out. I don't think Adams is going to have it after all. And it was my bottle."

She paused a moment, considering that the bottle could still be considered evidence. Well, if the police were doing their job—and Ted should know—then they found what they needed and already moved on.

"That sounds like an even better idea, although," she paused, remembering, "I've been known to get a little more than unwound drinking this stuff." More memories of Arvo, one in particular she wanted to completely forget flashed through her head. Of course she'd thought of Arvo immediately, how he might have looked into Adams' disappearance, what he would have done with the items left behind in her house. Also the numerous arguments that likely would have already broken out between them. The tension from the unhealed wounds.

The bourbon reminded her of why it had been the right decision to leave her job there, not that she was running away from her problems. From him. She was taking care of long overdue business, including getting her life back on course.

"Eh," Ted said dismissively. "You have nothing to worry about around here. You're on a sort of a vacation, right?"

"That's true," she said. "I am."

"Well, it's time to relax. You've earned it."

"You're right," she said, letting out the tension in a long sigh. "I've more than earned it."

"Keys?" he asked.

She quickly handed them over, and Ted set himself to work, driving first her car, then his truck, in. Once the autos were parked, he came in, and she poured out two small glasses of bourbon.

"Cheers," he said. "Happy vacationing."

"Cheers," she said, clinking his glass with hers. "Congratulations on your retirement."

They sipped bourbon together, looking out the window across the fields. It was four in the afternoon, and there was plenty of daylight left given it was nearly summer. The sun wouldn't be setting until well after 9:00 p.m.

"Well, I suppose we better get cracking if you're going to have a house that's clean enough to sleep in sometime tonight." While Ted hauled in her suitcases, Christine found the spare clothes she knew would be inside one of the bedroom dressers, got herself into an old cotton shirt and a worn pair of jeans, which both still fit her just as they had when she was in her late teens. The cedar lining of the dressers gave her a delightfully woodsy fragrance. She found the work boots right where she'd last left them in the bedroom closet. Her bedroom closet. She inspected them closely, noting that they were still in fine shape and only a light oiling would really make them perfect.

Adams had obviously not touched the second of the two bedrooms. Nothing had changed in the room from her last visit there. A stack of paperbacks she'd picked up at a yard sale, which were already dated when she was going through college and visiting her dad on summer break, sat neatly on the nightstand by the bed. She wasn't sure whether or not she had ever read the books—her dad kept her plenty busy over the summer—but she was glad to see she had a ready supply of light reading, so different from the heavy stacks of casework she usually read through at night. It looked like they'd offer some welcome distraction for the summer nights to come.

Still, since she wasn't quite sure when the sheets had last been washed, she stripped both of the beds. She went in search of Ted with an armload of sheets, and when he saw her coming down the hallway toward the laundry room, he chuckled.

"Now that's the Chrissy I know. Not that high maintenance city girl who arrived here an hour ago." He looked her up and down. "You look great!"

"So, that makes two of us wearing clothes we aren't used to being seen in. Trust me, *Christine* won't be gone for long. She's just on vacation." Christine liked the worn feel of her old clothes, but she felt almost unstable without the high heels and glamorous clothes she was used to. She foundered like a newborn foal, struggling to get her footing in flats. She knew how to deal with the world that demanded you wear fashion like it was armor. She felt defenseless in jeans and work boots. Maybe she'd have to resort to carrying around a handgun for a sense of security. She knew her dad had kept some tucked away in a safe in his closet. One that she alone had been given the combination to, though it was likely her dad had shared it with his buddy the cop.

Ted checked the water and assured Christine that the plumbing was working, and she tossed the sheets and bathroom towels into the washer. When a mouse ran out from under the washer, she didn't panic, at least not that she showed. Ted watched as she cornered it, then found a bucket to trap it, carrying it outside before it could scramble out.

"Need a spare cat?" Ted offered.

"I'm not really a cat person," she said. "Not really a dog person either, for that matter."

"Well, unless you want a lot of mousetraps around, a cat's your best bet."

"I'm not sure I want to take care of a pet," Christine said. At the moment she felt barely able to take care of herself.

"Cats take care of themselves. Ruth's cat had kittens a few months back. Maybe you need one here." Ruth was Ted's girlfriend. She'd been with him for almost twenty years, taking up with the widower who hadn't quit gotten over the loss of his wife to a drunk driver.

Lucid was part of lake country, and the town's population swelled in summer, as it had some of the finest bluegill fishing in the state. Along with the increase in vacationers, there came an increase in rowdy late nights at the local bars.

And that meant an increase in drunken driving.

Marie had been run down as she was crossing the county road on an evening walk. The hilly roads that led to town required extra care, as intersections and sudden curves in the road were common. Those unfamiliar with the roads could easily be startled by a sudden obstacle that appeared out of nowhere, even though there could be some benefit for the only auto repair shop in town. But even Buddy would have preferred not to have one wreck after another towed to his place.

Locals knew where to slow down and where you could comfortably and safely drive the speed limit. Visitors, particularly drunk drivers, didn't. Bad driving caused the worst of Ted's headaches, as well as his worst heartache.

The shock of Marie's death only hardened the resolve of some in Lucid, who had little respect for outsiders to begin with. It was bad enough that passers-through often left a trail of destruction, whether that was litter in campsites or garbage dumped on the roadways, but when the worst thing that could possibly happen ended up happening to the town cop—who ultimately couldn't protect the person dearest to him from the stupidity of an outsider—people's attitudes hardened even more than they had, which hardly seemed possible.

Ted and Ruth never got down to marrying, and even though people in a small town could be judgmental, given the circumstances of Marie's death, they showed respect for Ted and his deceased wife by keeping their nose out of Ted and Ruth's business.

Even if she was a couple decades younger than he was.

"There are two she hasn't found homes for yet."

"Two! Two cats to take care of? You're kidding me, right?"

"A couple are better than one. Trust me, they'll take care of themselves and your mouse problem. Your choice. Mousetraps and poison. Or a couple of cute kittens you'll fall in love with."

"What'll happen to them when I leave here?" Christine asked.

"You'll probably want to bring them with you. Or leave them with the next owner," he said with an inquisitive look.

"I haven't exactly decided to sell the place, just so you know." Christine turned away from him so he wouldn't be able to guess what she might be thinking. *She was pretty sure she was going to sell the place. She just wanted to figure out how to tell him.* She knew it would be hard for Ted to see his buddy's cherished place owned by someone else, possibly an outsider.

"If you do decide to sell it, it's probably a good time. With all of the speculation about shale oil, land prices have skyrocketed."

"Did Adams ever finish his report? Before he disappeared?"

"He told me he had, but I didn't pry about what he'd learned. Believe me, people around here were on pins and needles waiting to hear what he'd found out."

"So, nobody knows yet. Whether there's oil or not."

"Nope."

"I wonder if they'll have to start over with a new research team, to figure out whether there's oil or not." Christine had just emptied the rest of the rotting refrigerator contents left behind with Adams' sudden departure.

"That would really put people over the top. I talked to some people on his crew, when they came to town, since, basically I talk to everyone. The guy nearly drove everyone nuts with his demands for sampling." Ted hauled the overflowing garbage bag to his truck.

When he returned he was patting his stomach. "Judging by all the noise down here," Ted said, "it's way past dinner time. I should probably check in with Ruth, but then it's her bridge night, and I'm batching it anyway."

"How about I take you to the Y Not and buy you dinner?" Christine offered.

"Nice. A lady buying me dinner. Sounds like a perfect date to me."

"We'll consider it your belated retirement party. I'm sure if dad had been around, you'd have painted the town red. Just let me toss another load in the washer, then we can be on our way."

"Sure, I'll be out in the truck. Just come on out when you're ready." Ted grabbed another bag of garbage and headed out the door.

As soon as Christine had reloaded the washer and dryer, she checked her face in the bathroom and knew she had a little work to do on herself before she felt presentable, even at the Y Not. Thank goodness most of the redness from her crying had gone away. She knew Ted had seen the look of spent grief on her face. That might have been why he stayed as long as he did.

As she headed out the door, she noticed Adams's parka. She made a note on her to-do list that she needed to determine what, exactly, to do with it. "Don't get involved," she told herself. Maybe she'd just turn everything over to the Carlson County sheriff's office, since Ted was no longer involved with the ongoing investigation, and apparently had no interest in pursuing it, even out of curiosity.

For now she hung the guy's jacket on the coat stand behind the door. The Jim Beam bottle had already been put away in a cupboard. She knew all of the stuff should be turned over to the county, but when she thought about it, even she wasn't interested having any cops crawling all over her property, asking questions, when all of that should have been done months before.

She crossed the task off her list, added a checkmark next to the crossed off task, and wrote DONE in bold capital letters there as well.

"Chrissy, Chrissy," Ted scolded when she appeared at the passenger side of his truck in a fresh outfit. She'd done her best to tone down her usual night-out wardrobe of form-fitting mini-dresses and heels.

"What?" she asked, climbing inside, though she knew very well what was bothering him. In moments, she'd transformed herself from a grubby farm girl Chrissy to the chic, albeit restrained, Christine. She had dressed down (or so she thought) in a pair of low-riding skinny green jeans and an animal print knit top, accented by a plain caramel-colored leather belt, ballerina flats and a small clutch. She'd used minimal make-up, and moussed-up her super short haircut.

"Really. You looked fine," Ted said. "I'll admit, you look like a super-model in those clothes, very nice. But you should save those duds for the city. We're a blue-jeans-and-flannel-shirt sort of crowd."

"Eh," she said, "It'll be fine. Don't worry." Christine didn't want to be seen in blue jeans and a flannel shirt for her first night in Lucid in years. She needed her armor, as much as she could load on. She didn't know what to expect—whether Lucid would consider her one of their own, or an outsider. She figured the latter was more likely.

"Dressed like that I should be taking you to the Pelican Falls Applebee's, not the Y Not."

"The Y Not will be just fine," she said. "And, remember, I'm taking you out. It's your retirement party."

"Suit yourself," he finally said, turning the ignition key and starting the engine. "I'll be hearing about this for days," he said.

"You know how these people are." He glanced at her again, with an apprehensive look in his eye.

"Since when have you been afraid of being ribbed by the crew down at Y Not?" she asked him. "Aren't they still more scared of you, considering everything you know about everybody's business? I mean you know where all the bodies are buried," she said lightly, remembering that there was one person whose whereabouts he should know, but didn't. She dropped the subject.

He began driving down the gravel road, the familiar sounds of black walnut fruits crunching underneath his tires, accented by the pinging of gravel spun up by his wheels. Those sounds accentuated the awkward silence that suddenly fell between them.

"You know," Ted said as they came to the county road, "it used to be more light-hearted in town, but things have changed around here from what you remember. Farming's always a tough profession, and really there's not much else to the economy around here than farming. And so you always have more have-nots than haves. But the talk of oil really got people whipped up."

"I don't believe for one second that there's any oil here," Christine said, glancing at her face in the passenger-side visor mirror.

"How do you know?" Ted said, turning off the driveway onto the county road. "There were teams of people crawling all over the countryside all last summer, taking samples and sending truckloads of stuff out of here. You should have seen the money they were throwing around town. No one blinked when their bar tab, even at the Y Not, would go into the hundreds of dollars. The waitresses were making huge tips. I was really starting to worry about what all the money was going to do to our crime rate. That was partly why it was easy to finally hang up my badge and turn in my gun."

"So, it's a lot of speculation. It'll all die down soon enough and life will go on as usual."

"See, that's the thing."

Christine screwed her lipstick down, snapped the cover back on, and tossed it in her purse. She gave him the beat or two he needed to make his point.

"It hasn't died down," he said. "If anything it's gotten worse."

"Well, didn't this missing geologist turn in his final report? Maybe his company just hasn't made anything public yet."

"No," he said. "Everything, including his final report, went missing with him."

They drove on through the rolling countryside, the muddy and just greening farm fields that Christine tried hard to imagine covered with a new farm implement: drilling rigs. She still thought it sound too far-fetched.

"So, this guy didn't email it to anyone? Or save it on his computer?"

"Computer's missing along with the guy," Ted said.

Christine knew enough from her experience working alongside detectives that there were other places where electronic files could be saved. She'd stood behind analysts, remembering one quite fondly, a reed-thin, redheaded young man with thick glasses named Kieran—only Kieran—a crafty code-lover who went by just one name.

"AND I SUPPOSE THIS GUY DIDN'T SAVE his research on the company computer drives somewhere?" Christine said, still thinking of Kieran, the crack researcher with an ability to locate anything you needed in thirty seconds or less, usually faster. He would have found a copy of this report months ago and saved everyone the grief they seemed to be experiencing in Lucid.

"Drives? What? Hell, Chrissy! I'm a small town cop. Ruthie's son might understand what you're talking about, but not me. When I retired, I filed my last reports the same way I'd done it for decades. On paper."

They turned onto Lucid's Main Street. Main Street stretched from a 1920s era high school to a century-old grain elevator, with a dozen storefronts, many empty, mounded up haphazardly on the main drag as if plowed together by a lunatic on a Bobcat.

Angled summer sunlight stretched fun house shadows of the Y Not Restaurant, the post office, the bank, the beauty shop, the Quik Cleen laundromat, a tiny grocery store and the other sparsely appointed shops lining the road. That confirmed what Christine thought as she passed by town on her way in: nothing had changed from the Lucid she'd known ten years before. She wondered if Ted's opinions of how Lucid had changed were overblown. Ted's truck passed through the misshapen shadows, the dark judgment of evening falling across the town.

"A computer drive is like an electronic safe deposit box. Once a person saves files on a hard drive, it's almost impossible for it to disappear, even if the file gets erased. What's this company he worked for?"

Yes. Kieran would have found something by now. But he was a few hundred miles and several hours southeast of Lucid. In Mendota County. In a life she'd left behind, determined never to return to.

"Never mind," she said, reminding herself again that one of the reasons she was in Lucid was to put Mendota County behind her. "I don't want to know. All I want now is one of the Y Not's famous Salisbury steaks. Maybe a beer."

They parked in front of the Y Not. "Okay," he said. "We're officially done talking about missing geologists then. But before we go in there, I need to warn you again. Things have changed in Lucid. It's not the same place you knew ten years ago. It may look the same from the outside, but things have changed. I'm still sorry your dad's gone, but I'm not sure how he would've handled all of this oil business. I mean, you get it don't you?"

"Get what?" she asked.

"Chrissy," he said with an almost pleading tone to his voice. "People are in limbo here without that guy's final report giving either the thumbs up or thumbs down for oil. Until we know, one way or another, people are kind of on edge. And, the thing is . . ." he hesitated.

"What . . . Ted? What exactly?" she said, waiting to hear the point of where he was headed.

"You're sitting on top of a whole section of prime land out there. Even before this oil rumor started, I had people coming after me asking if you wanted to sell. And I knew you hadn't decided. So, I said 'no' for you, and kept renting it out to be farmed, sending you the rental checks, a tidy sum, as you know, regularly."

No, she didn't know. The money went straight into an account she didn't look at. She'd buried it when she buried her dad, not wanting to think too long or too hard about what the loss meant to her.

Ted went on. "Chrissy, let me be as clear as I can be. All the people inside town here—with very few exceptions—are the have-nots. We're just scraping by out here. The oil people helped quite a bit last summer for those with businesses in town, but now they're gone and the future's uncertain. So, for most of town, an oil find could do something to improve the economy, maybe help some people go from just getting by to actually turning a decent profit. Though of course there's a downside. And I'd already seen that downside cropping up here and there. People looking to make a fast buck. Grab their piece of the action, and not in completely legal ways. The pressure's on, for everyone, and particularly for people just scraping to get by. Then there are a few in a different category. And you're one of them."

Christine had always felt different from the people of Lucid, but she had hoped things might be better for her in a place where her family had roots. "So why am I 'one of them'?" she asked.

"At today's farmland prices, you're sitting on several million dollars worth of land. A whole section, girl. If you sold it as farmland, you could easily never have to work again. Just live off what you made from selling it, though, of course, you might have to shop a little less for your expensive duds."

"I get them second-hand, at a consignment shop, just so you know," she said, feeling slightly embarrassed. "So probably my lifestyle wouldn't change much." To think of never working again was mind-blowing. Though she'd likely go crazy without a job to keep her busy organizing and scheduling.

"That's the Chrissy I know. Thrifty like your dad. You know a bargain when you see it and wait for the right price. That doesn't make you like the rest of us though. See, you're one of the haves. Your dad made that happen for you, and as far as Lucid is concerned, he became one of us again, even though he spent a lot of years in the city. And even though he got himself in a great position out here, he didn't boast about it or act like a show off. People liked your dad."

"Oh, I know that." She felt a few tears forming in her eyes.

"But to Lucid, you're an outsider now. Even though your dad was born and raised here, you weren't. You were this rich college-educated girl who got lucky having an old man who did well. You haven't spent time in town in ages. I'm just saying that now that you're back, watch out. If this geologist and/or his report turn up, the pressure's only going to be worse."

Crap, she thought again, wondering if she made the wrong decision coming to Lucid and hoping for a break from stress. It was bad enough coming to town to deal with memories of her father as she decided what to do with his property. Now all this oil business. She examined her lipstick one more time, applying another coat of bright red armor.

"I'll be fine," she said, knowing she had been in the past. Even though her nerves were already frayed, she repeated. "I'll be fine. I can take care of myself." She looked at Ted's face, seeing the same worried expression her father used to have when he thought

Christine was pushing herself too hard. When she was determined to go it alone, and not ask for help.

"Don't even worry about it, Ted. In fact, I'm sorry you've had all of this on your shoulders. I'm here now, at last. I should've been up here years ago, figuring out what to do and taking the pressure off of you. You had plenty to do in your job."

"I took it all on," he said, "Gladly. Best buddy meant the world to me. Got me out of more than a few scrapes, helped me when I lost my wife. I owe him."

"Well, you've more than paid your dues. It's my turn to handle my dad's stuff." She saw customers exiting the Y Not, nodding at Ted, glancing at her, trying not to look too long.

"Well, are you ready? Got that lipstick right yet?"

"You bet," she said. "Let's just forget all about this oil business tonight. Relax a bit."

"Whatever you say, Chrissy." He exited the truck while she gathered her things, but before she could get out on her own, he was there ready to open the door for her. She opened it herself in a hurry and scurried out. It was the first sign she gave that she intended to take care of herself, to show that she knew she'd be fine. She almost knocked him over with the car door.

"Well, you certainly know how to show a fella you mean business," he said, a little wearily.

"Um. Sorry about that." She probably should have let him open the door for her.

"Your dad and I were raised to be gentlemen, you know, open doors for ladies and all," he said, as Christine stepped out onto Main Street. "You can be a lady, occasionally you know, and let a guy help you out."

Christine was not sure this was the time she should show any amount of need for a man's assistance. She threw back her shoulders and stood arrow straight, walking with as much confidence as she could in ballerina flats. She almost wished she'd gone with her first instinct, and thrown on the pair of stiletto-heeled shortie boots she'd brought along. Definitely next time.

When they got to the door of the Y Not, this time she did pause and let Ted open it for her. She may as well make an entrance into the Lucid social scene, no holds barred. She thought she saw a brief look of apprehension in Ted's eyes, once more, before entering the Y Not. But she put it out of her mind. There was Salisbury steak to be ordered and eaten. One or two beers to wash it back. No matter what anyone in Lucid thought, she had a right to be here, as much as anyone else.

This was her father's hometown, and she owned a substantial piece of land on the edge of town. No one was going to stop her from doing what she needed to do, and making her decisions in her own way and in her own time. It had taken ten years for her to get to this point—she was not going to throw it all away, driven by oil speculation and town gossip fueled by envious have-nots.

3

CHRISTINE IVORY MADE AN ENTRANCE, but not the one she'd hoped for. She had the strange sensation that people had been anticipating her arrival at the Y Not, judging by the fact that every head was turned to the doorway with an expectant look on each face. She knew Ted hadn't called ahead and made reservations. The only phone in the place was a non-operating coin phone, yet to be replaced with a credit card version. The phone company had obviously not gotten around to it and had no plans to get around to it anytime soon.

As much as Ted had warned her that things had changed, the one thing that hadn't changed was the Y Not. It was a long narrow room lined down one side with high-backed wooden booths and a countertop over a display case of pies, cakes, and other pastries facing a small bar, on the opposite side. Above the bar, display cases of taxidermied ducks, geese, and other field birds, which hadn't been added to over Christine's lifetime, presided just below the painted tin ceiling. A modest salad bar was tucked at the end of the room, and several Formica-topped tables were lined up in the center of the room. Off behind the salad bar, a long banquette lined the far wall. This was where farmers gathered routinely during the growing season, and hunters held court the rest of the year.

Ted led her to one of the booths, and once Christine slid in, Ted quietly spoke.

"See what I mean?" Ted said.

"You mean they don't go silent and stare at everyone who walks in?" Christine said quietly. She'd remembered a much different reception at her last visit to the Y Not. Friendly hellos from everyone. But then she'd been with her dad, and she was a kid home from college.

"Not exactly." Ted looked uncomfortable. Maybe it was up to her to break the ice. She could put on her professional self, and be ready for anything. She'd been used to a hostile reception in her profession, given her clientele. She'd dealt with Mendota County's most troubled kids. Some were young victims of the worst kinds of abuse and she'd been able to turn lives around when no one else could. Despite that thick skin she'd developed helping children recover from the inhumanity they'd encountered, she wasn't sure what was going to work with people who'd known her almost her entire life. So what if she'd been gone awhile, changed a little. She was still Rob Ivory's daughter.

Dolly the waitress dropped by, nodding at Ted, saying nothing to Christine. "Today's specials are meatloaf or roast beef. If that doesn't interest you, I can bring a menu."

Ted thought it best to go with the specials. "Chrissy would like the meatloaf. I'll take the roast beef," he said.

"I'd like the Salisbury steak," Christine piped up, "Though I know the meatloaf and it's great. I just had my heart set on the steak."

Dolly gave her a wary look. "Salisbury steak it is," she said, not writing anything on her pad.

"I'd like a beer, too," Christine continued, even though the waitress had turned her back and already started heading away. "Please?" The waitress returned and took their drink orders.

"How's Bill?" Ted asked. "That ankle of his recover yet?" Ted broke the ice for her.

"He's still having a hard time getting around," Dolly said. "He could definitely use some time on a boat. Every time he hears the fish are biting, his mood drops."

"Tell him I'd be glad to come out to your place and get him out on the lake. I still owe him for that plumbing work he did at the police station, years ago. When the toilet went out in our cell and we had that ornery, half-crazy druggie guy in there with the bad case of food poisoning. Real explosive situation, if you know what I mean." Bill was the town plumber.

"Sure, I'll tell him. That will cheer him right up." Dolly said, eyeing Christine. "How long are you back?"

Christine was surprised by the blunt question, and realized since she herself didn't know, it was unlikely that the grapevine had anything to pass along to Dolly in that regard.

She and Dolly were roughly the same age, though Dolly looked a good ten years older. Dolly was short and heavyset. In her youth, she'd been one of the town's hot young things, on the wild side, a cute and curvy brunette with sparkling eyes. Christine knew Dolly's husband Bill, as well.

Back in the day, he'd been quite the catch. He had a baseball scholarship at Morris, but after high school his batting average and grades dropped. He'd had a hard time concentrating—his borderline attention deficit disorder never diagnosed, except by Christine, years later after she'd earned her degree and came back to Lucid for the occasional visit. Christine had never said anything, and with her education opening her eyes wide to the true conditions of some of Lucid's residents, she quickly spotted what had held Bill back all these years.

"I don't really know yet, to be honest." She thought the disclosure might make her seem approachable. She even smiled.

Dolly took that single statement as enough polite conversation from Christine. "I'll go place your order now. Be back with your drinks in a jif."

"Say hello . . ." she began, but Dolly quickly placed herself out of earshot. Dolly wasn't interested in passing along a greeting from Christine to Dolly's husband Bill. Bill had dropped out of the University of Minnesota at Morris after only one year, coming back to Lucid to find work in his father's plumbing business. He and Dolly married the next summer, and by then, she had already given birth to their first baby. Christine had been invited to the combo bridal/baby shower and the wedding. She declined both invitations, claiming a schedule conflict. Her father told her later that Dolly probably felt snubbed by her. That judgment wasn't quite fair, since Christine was attending an out-of-state college and not able to visit Lucid at the drop of a hat.

"I'm proud of you, Chrissy," her father had told her once. "But you have to look at things from the Lucid perspective. They also might be proud, but what they see is that you've chosen a life as far away from here as you can get."

"You and my dad are natives," Christine said to Ted, exactly the same point she'd made with her dad, years earlier. "And I'm not, I know. But why do they even have the right to judge me?"

"That's the small-town mentality for you," Ted said. "It took your dad a couple of years to get accepted around here again, when he bought that place up on the hill. They'd come around, and accept you too, if you were here more often."

She doubted that.

Dolly efficiently, and a little robotically, handed them their open beers. "May I have a glass?" Christine asked.

Dolly's wary look now bordered on anger. "Sure thing," she said, not actually sounding like she meant it.

"Really?" Ted said to her when Dolly went for a glass. "You couldn't just drink it out of a bottle?"

"Sorry," Christine said. "I kind of have a slight phobia about bottles." And a number of other compulsions she didn't want to mention. She was hoping that time in the country would help cure her obsessive nature, the aftereffect from her high-pressure life. To cleanse herself from days spent in her clients' chaotic lives, she'd grown more and more obsessed with having a clean, organized environment outside of work.

She knew some of her tendencies made her borderline OCD, especially when they kept her from being fully functional or delayed her from getting to important business. It was another reason she'd taken some time away from the job. She was hoping that she could loosen up. She already thought she'd been loose enough, given how the day had gone. She hadn't even shrieked when she saw the mouse, though she planned on disinfecting the kitchen one more time tonight yet.

"The Chrissy I knew never had that kind of problem."

"That Chrissy is a good twenty years in the past."

"I liked that girl. She's welcome back, anytime," Ted said.

Christine felt as if she'd been slapped. "What about Christine? Isn't she welcomed back?"

Christine's glass had not appeared, and given the turn in the conversation, she felt it necessary to make a statement. She took a long swig out of her bottle, then set it down firmly on the table. The loud smack of glass against Formica countertop startled nearby customers. Everyone turned to stare.

"Now, now, Chrissy. I was just joking." He smiled and greeted the staring customers. "Hey Bob. Fred. How's it going?"

Fred and Bob nodded, then turned back to their own conversations.

"Seriously. I've never seen you so on edge in all the years I've known you. What has gotten you so rattled?"

Christine groaned and raked her fingers through her short, spiky hair. She held her head in her fingertips, staring down at the tabletop, remembering the expensive yoga instructor's words. What was her mantra? She'd forgotten, abandoning yoga after only a few sessions. It only made her feel more tense. She couldn't spare the time it took to take yoga in order to help her to learn how to relax. She didn't have time to relax.

She looked up into Ted's face, wondering how much she could push him until he really did finally lose it with her.

"Okay. For the third time today, I'm sorry. Honestly, I'm not entirely sure what has gotten into me." She took another long swig of her beer, nearly emptying it. "I really thought it would be different, coming up here."

"Different? How?" Ted asked, motioning to Dolly to bring them both another. Dolly returned, this time with a glass for Christine.

"Thank you," Christine said to Dolly, before answering Ted's questions. "I don't know. I thought once I got far away from the city, all of my problems would magically melt away. Instead, they seem to be worse than ever."

"What kind of problems have you been having?" Ted asked quietly.

"I suppose I shouldn't be talking so loudly about this. Everyone already knows everything about me, and I don't need to give them more material to work with," she said, glancing at Bob and Fred, who were still occasionally glancing in their direction.

"Really. You don't have to go into it if you don't want to," Ted said.

"No," Christine said. "It's fine. I'll just try to be a bit more discreet." She poured her beer into the glass, waiting a few moments for the foam to subside. "Basically, I guess I just got burnt out. The last two high profile cases I was on really got to me."

"Yeah, we heard about them all the way up here. The babies that had washed up on the beaches? The one that the little girl found?"

"Yes, that one especially. And a few others."

"But you handled those cases, and more over the years. How did it manage to get to you, tough as nails Christine, who, I will admit, I am starting to like more and more. Though I still miss Chrissy." He reached across the table and patted her hand.

She smiled.

"So what happened?" he said.

"I got involved," she said, surprising herself that she was admitting it, "with the lead detective."

"Now that news didn't get all the way here," he said with a wink. "So the grapevine isn't foolproof."

"Thank god for that," she said, clinking her glass against his bottle. "Cheers for the downfall of the grapevine."

"What was the guy's name? We saw his picture in the papers. Not a great looking guy, but seemed likable enough."

She girded herself to say his name out loud, for the first time in months. "Thorson. Arvo Thorson." There, she had said it and her voice didn't break once. Maybe she was finally making some progress.

"Oh, yeah, that's right. He brought that senator down, didn't he?"

"Yup. That was him. And he brought down even more movers and shakers with the most recent case, in a case that expanded across county lines."

"Yes. It's coming back to me now. Sounds like an impressive sort of fellow. Good cop, so of course he has my respect. So, I'm guessing things didn't work out?" he said quietly.

She shook her head, thankful to be able to avert her eyes from Ted's to the approaching Dolly's. She did not want him to see her eyes welling up, to her frustration. She and Arvo had no business in a relationship with each other, and now he seemed quite happily involved with someone else.

Dolly approached their table with two steaming entrées, setting the Salisbury steak in front of Christine and the roast beef in front of Ted. Given the amount of brown gravy covering both entries, each with matching sides of mashed potatoes and string beans, the plates almost looked identical.

Christine took a few bites and despite the appearance, was rewarded by the homey taste she remembered. She allowed herself a moment of revelry in the heavy, salty flavor, bland where she wanted bland. After a few moments, she felt calm enough to go on.

"To close the loop on this Arvo thing," she said, the light tone sounding ridiculous the moment she began, "we have known each other a long, long time. Don't get me wrong: the guy is great at what he does. Though his style leaves a lot to be desired." She knew by now that had it been Arvo across the table from her, he'd already have gravy splotches on his shirt. Christine knew that she was a touch, well way too much, on the tidy and neat side. But Arvo was a bona fide slob. Still, she wanted to be charitable in explaining him to Ted, and also accept her share of the blame.

"So, it was one of those things where you were just too different from each other to make it work?"

"Something like that," she said, imagining Arvo across the table again. A smile crossed Ted's face, and she imagined Arvo grinning, which he had from time to time.

"He's already moved on to someone else," she said. "And it really hardly got started between us before it was over." That was stretching it a bit. They were involved for practically a year. Until he did the unforgiveable and fell in bed with his ex-wife, the conniving bitch.

"Well, it sounds like one of those things that wasn't going to work out. I got lucky with Ruthie, that's for sure."

"The two of you have been together a long time now," she said, "haven't you?"

"Twenty years. We've had our ups and downs, just like everyone else, I guess," Ted said.

Christine wondered if there was a reason why they'd never gotten married, given the length of their relationship. Perhaps the downs were worse than he was admitting.

"Of course, you can pretty much expect she'll be out to see you, first thing in the morning," he said between bites of roast beef and forkfuls of mashed potatoes.

"Yeah, I was expecting that. Probably a whole line of curiosity seekers wondering what I'm up to at Dad's place." She polished off her steak and began to work on the mound of potatoes.

"Better prepare yourself with some answers, unless you want to be constantly asked about your plans," he said. "You must be used to being questioned when you are working with the witnesses right? You coach them about what to say and everything?"

"Well, actually, I really can't do that. That would really blow a case, as you would probably know. I just try to help them to be ready, to know what kinds of things they'll be asked, how long it will take. I help them to deal with all sorts of tough situations, without actually telling them what to do."

"Well, that sounds like good preparation for what you might face here, given the missing geologist and the oil madness. Everyone thinks the reason the guy wanted to rent your dad's—I mean *your* place—is that he thought there might be a huge find out there."

"It still sounds like a whole lot of foolish speculation. How ridiculous."

"I'm just trying to help you understand how big of a deal this is."

She found herself thinking that had this all gone down in Mendota County, the guy would have been located by now, dead or alive. Though she had respect for Ted as a police officer. But she wasn't in Mendota County.

"I get it. People are going to be asking me a lot of questions. Tell you what," she said, taking her last bite. "Once I know what I'm up to out there, I'll put out a press release and save everyone the trouble of asking."

"Well, let me know first," Ted said. "I'll be able to tell you how people will react to the news."

"Sure thing," she said as Dolly walked by.

"May I have the check?" Christine asked.

"Ted already covered it," she said.

"I wanted to treat Robby's girl," he explained.

"Well, considering how many times I wound up apologizing to you today, I'm surprised you still think that." She shook her head.

"Not much of choice," he said, "considering you remind me a lot of your dad."

"Well, I find that pretty hard to believe, but I'll accept the compliment. Next time let me earn the treat," she said as they left the Y Not. "Judging by today, I have a lot of work on my hands."

"You bet, Chrissy. You bet."

4

CHRISTINE SENT TED HOME AFTER HE dropped her off at her place, telling him several times she could handle the remaining chores herself. He promised to stop by with a kitten or two in the next day, unless Ruthie beat him out there in the morning. She told him again she didn't know if she wanted to take care of a pet. He said, unless she considered mice pets, she really had no choice. It was mice or cats, take her pick.

She chose cats. She wondered whether she would survive, fearing she'd be thought of as a weird old cat spinster, and resolved to get her hair freshened up and her nails manicured as soon as she could. No one was going to see her and think cat spinster, of that she was absolutely certain.

There was still daylight left, even though it was approaching 8:00 p.m. She watched Ted drive the entire length of the driveway, watched until he had turned onto the county road, and until the truck disappeared into the dip of the road near where a small stream cut through her property, the outlet stream from a small pair of spring-fed twin lakes deep in one of the folds in the land.

She knew exactly where the spring was, having swum in the little lakes many times in her teens. Air temperatures could reach a hundred, or more, in the summertime, in the temperamental climate of the prairie. Her dad had kept a rusty old truck for her use, teaching her to drive it when she wasn't quite teenaged, and when the temperature demanded it, she drove it by herself across the rutted farm fields to take a swim in the deliciously cold section near the northern shoreline, close to where the twin lakes were joined by a narrow channel. That same area of the twin lakes never quite froze in winter, offering a continuous fresh water source to deer that wintered in the woods that surrounded the land there.

She wondered if conditions might get that hot during her time in Lucid. She wondered if some remnant of that teenage girl was still inside her, the one unafraid of walking through the slippery mud along the shoreline, the girl who wasn't creeped out by the sight of a leech clinging to a spot between her toes.

She hoped it got hot enough to find out. That old truck was long gone, but Christine knew it had been replaced by a newer version, which was likely still parked exactly where it had been in the pole barn. Another task on her list for the days ahead.

Before she went back inside, she realized that it would be her first night alone there, in her entire life. And even though she was a single woman (and *not* a batty, cat-crazy spinster, she told herself), and had spent the majority of her nights alone (by her choice), somehow it seemed different in Lucid. Her dad had always been there. In fact, it was the only place where she was never alone at night. For the first time, she would experience loneliness in a place where she'd always found good company. Security. Love and affection even when she didn't deserve it, but needed it.

Christine found that the sheets and towels were completely dry, and she took her time folding and hanging the towels with the meticulousness she'd drilled into herself: precise, board-flat thirds. The activity relaxed her more than any amount of alcohol might have. Organizing and cleaning always had that effect on her.

She made the bed in the little room, noticing that the cheap permanent press sheets her father bought didn't need the ironing required for her expensive, imported Pima cotton sheets at home. But they would be nowhere near as comfortable. And it was too late for a late night run to the Pelican Falls Fleet Farm, where she might at least find a polyester cotton blend. She knew her standards were ridiculous, even in the city, even though she could afford better. She was in the country. The same sheets had been used on her bed for years, while her expensive sheets had to be replaced every few years.

Though the cleaning and tidying had brought her blood pressure back to its normal low, she made herself stop working after she'd mopped the kitchen and bathroom floors one more time, scoured the sink, wiped down every countertop, the inside of the refrigerator, and swept off the porch. She finally considered herself done for the evening around 11:00 p.m., so she locked up and got ready for bed. Since she hadn't gotten the tub cleaned out, a sponge bath would have to do.

The fresh but worn bathroom towels felt wonderful though not terribly absorbent on her sweaty skin. She didn't even bother to wait until the water heated up in the bathroom. The cool rough washcloth took off both the grime and the remains of her makeup, and when she looked at herself in the mirror, she saw how worn she was getting.

A good night's sleep in a clean bed was sure to get everything back in order. She wondered if she had time to run up to Pelican Falls the next day and get herself a few makeup items, maybe some wrinkle cream. Then she made herself promise not to do anything of the kind. It was time to work on obsessing *less* over her appearance. Lucid seemed the perfect place to experiment with a more carefree regime. Carefree for Christine that is. The day she went without any kind of cosmetic would probably be the day she should check into the Pelican Falls Asylum, though the old facility had, she knew, been closed many years.

She crawled into bed wearing an old high school jersey from Somerset Hills as her pajamas. She laughed when she saw herself in the mirror that hung above the dresser. Her graduation year was crackled and faded off in places, and with her make-up scrubbed off her face, she caught a brief glimpse of her younger self almost completely hidden by too many wrinkled years of stress: all the youthful sharpnesss had cracked and faded like the year from the jersey. In those days, the path ahead was the big bold font. Now, nothing was quite that clear. Another sign of how life was moving on. Christine hoped she would grow more comfortable in her own worn skin, maybe by the time summer was over and the new job was starting.

As she sat in bed just listening to the silence of the house, she realized she'd forgotten how quiet it got in the country, and even though she was exhausted, her nerves were so fried that she couldn't immediately drop off to sleep. She selected a paperback at random out of the pile on the nightstand. Thankfully she'd selected James Clavell's *Noble House*, a story of British and Chinese businessmen struggling over a trading house, over the murder mystery *Gorky Park*. She'd spotted a Harold Robbins best seller from the early 1980s in the pile, and laughed at the taste of her younger self. For a moment she thought of picking it up instead of the Clavell, knowing how lurid Robbins's writing could be. But she didn't need more excitement, even Robbins's style, keeping her awake much longer.

She looked at the windows. Though they were high on the wall in her bedroom and since the house was on top of a hill in the middle of farm fields, her father had never bothered to put in curtains. She hadn't much cared when she was younger, but too many years of working with crime victims had made her wary. She knew how unlikely it was she'd have problems, but bad things happened everywhere, even way out in the sticks. She planned to get window coverings up, first thing in the morning. She made a note on a little pad on the bed stand.

The wind came up after dark, rushing up and around the rolling hillside, and she remembered hearing on the drive up that the weather might get bad overnight. But the sound of the wind didn't frighten her. In fact, she felt comforted by the hush it made through the trees. Though high winds and storms could be threatening, she wasn't the only person threatened by it. The fact that havoc could reign without discrimination, and not solely be dumped on her, helped her feel calm again.

She fell asleep with the light on, flitting in and out of sleep and constantly thinking she should try and wake up enough to shut the light off. At some point she did, not completely remembering when, and fell into a disturbing dream that her Lucid house was surrounded by townspeople trying to peek through the windows at her. She walked from room to room in her dream, continuing the cleaning she hadn't finished during the day, to occasionally look up and see Dolly or Bill or any of the other people in the town of 500 staring at her through her windows. Ted sat calmly on the porch sipping a cup of coffee. Next to him, her father sat, a cup in his hand as well. They chatted to each other without seeming to notice that the porch was surrounded by hundreds of people, all pressed up against the screens.

More and more kept coming up, pressing their faces against the glass, and in her dream Christine kept cleaning even though she was unnerved by the great number of people pressed against the house. She opened the front door with a bag of garbage in her hand, but the screen door was blocked by townspeople, trapping her inside. Their mouths were moving, but not a word came out. All the while, Ted and her father continued their own little conversation, not noticing the crowds building around them, not noticing her distress.

Finally, the people pressed so close that the porch screens began to rip. The tearing sound it made was so loud that Christine actually woke up in terror. She sat straight up in bed, her heart pounding, and it took her a few moments to realize that she was indeed awake, that it had all been a dream. She listened to the sound of the wind, still blowing just the same as it had been when she had drifted off to sleep. The little digital clock on the dresser blinked 12:00, and she knew that it wasn't actually 12:00. She simply hadn't set it. She settled back into the sheets, waiting for the fast tick of her heart to slow, and just as she started to drift off again, she heard another tearing sound.

Apparently that part of her dream had been real after all.

She switched on the bedside lamp, sat up, and slid her bare feet into the work boots, and in her hurry to investigate she didn't take the time to tie the laces. Most likely it was an animal trying to work its way inside the screen porch, she told herself. What else could it be? She still felt terrorized by her dream, but pushed the thought of it out of her head as best she could. Probably the dream had been fed by the sound of late-night animals. She walked through the tiny spare room off the main living room area, a room that had functioned as both family room and guest room, though was never used for guests, as no one but her father and herself ever used the place. A small black-and-white television set sat on a side table, and the old hard sofa bed, which had never been opened, sat under a dustcover. She switched the deadbolt for the door leading to the screened porch, thankful she'd remembered to lock it before heading to bed.

Her heart was pounding again, wondering whether she should even investigate further. Who knew what might have gotten into the screen porch.

Well, Christine, she thought, *you better learn how to deal with this, even if it's only going to be for a couple of weeks.* Why she was all of a sudden scared of being alone, and in the dark, heavens knew. This was the country for God's sake. All kinds of critters were active at night. She remembered how her dad had to store the garbage cans in the pole barn, since the raccoons had tipped them over so many times before. And hadn't she left a bag of the rotting stuff she'd tossed from the fridge in the screen porch? Possibly? Though she was certain Ted had hauled everything away. Still, who knew?

She took a breath, turned on the flashlight, and opened the door to the screen porch. Just as she got it open, she heard the scuttle of claws across the porch floor and her flashlight caught the bright eyes of baby raccoons, hurrying away after their mother through the hole they'd chewed through a screen near the door.

She laughed at the sight of the furry little devils, waddling away as fast as they could. She searched around and sure enough, there was a chewed open garbage bag, the remains of some rotted lunch-meat container they'd been feasting on.

"Well," she said aloud, pleased by the sound of her own voice. She'd survived after all. The dream goblins had been fed into her sleeping consciousness by a family of masked, furry, nighttime bandits.

She had a mess to clean up before she could go back to bed. The screen repair would have to wait, obviously, until morning. But the raccoon bait would have to go. She found an empty garbage bag in the kitchen, put on a pair of rubber gloves, and picked up the rest of the mess, breathing through her mouth to avoid the stink.

After retrieving the pole barn key from the house, she headed off with a flashlight in one hand, the garbage in the other.

She quickly learned that a woman could be sure of herself in six-inch stiletto heels, but outdone by navigation over uneven ground, covered with lime-sized black walnut fruits in untied work boots. She fell down hard on her knees, banging her wrists on the rough ground, swearing in the same colorful language her father always reserved for such occasions. She rubbed her smarting knees, shining the flashlight on them to inspect the damage.

Just then a car door slammed, not far away. Her instincts still sharp, she scrambled to her feet.

A pair of bright red taillights lit up at the distant end of the driveway. Moments later, a car sped off the last remaining feet of her driveway, speeding away from her place, and town, in the dead of the night.

"What the hell?" she said to no one. Replaying those events a moment or two later, she remembered other sounds proceeded the car door slam. She recalled the sound of footsteps, hurried ones, running away from the house on the gravel road.

Was it possible that something other than raccoons had tried breaking into her house? She left the garbage where it was and hobbled quickly back inside, swearing at no one in particular that she had no time to lace the work boots. She grabbed her keys, and hurried back to the car, her automatic professional reaction to the events still triggering her. Though not a cop, she'd been around them enough, been involved in enough witness interviews and court cases to be programmed to evaluate any potential crime scene details. Even when bad guys may, or may not be, involved. Intruders had been on her property and she was damned if she was going to let them threaten what she hoped might be a peaceful few weeks in the country.

She sped down her own driveway, turning the direction the strange vehicle had turned, and saw its taillights crest a distant hill north on the county road.

Not even out of the job for a few days and here I am again. This time she didn't attempt to make herself forget all about her recent past. She had property to defend, and an intruder was getting away.

But her city-driving skills were no match for someone more familiar with the undulating roads of the post-glacial landscape. It wasn't long before she lost sight of the other car. She turned around and headed back to the house. By the time she got the garbage stowed away in the pole barn, a summer morning was making itself known in a slowly brightening sky and birdsong. She was too wound up to go back to sleep anyway. She unpacked her expensive single-cup coffee machine and brewed the first of many cups that day, keeping watch from a chair inside the screen house until long past dawn, making a long list of unexpected tasks:

among them, screen repair, installation of motion detector lighting, and perhaps even a security system with cameras.

She intended to have some sense of peace before her head hit the pillow the next night, and she would need every hour of daylight to get that security and peace she had been craving for weeks.

5

By noon, Christine's stomach was growling. She'd skipped breakfast, and had about an hour before she was expecting the arrival of the security company she'd found in Pelican Falls. She knew she was going to have to pay their most expensive rate, but the cost was equal to the price of her peace of mind, and while she bargained them down a bit by packaging some extra services, it was still far more than she would have paid in Mendota County for similar services.

But she knew she'd have to pay. It was twenty miles to Pelican Falls, the closest mid-sized city in the area. She had no other choice. Had she been able to wait a few days, she might have gotten a better deal on the installation charge. But she didn't want to wait.

There was still the torn screen, which, since it was on the screen porch and the actual entry to the house from the porch was secured by a dead-bolted, steel door, it seemed less of a worry for human intruders. As long as she made sure that garbage didn't get left in the screen porch, she felt relatively safe from humans and could deal with occasional invasion from raccoons.

The sight of a car turning up her driveway caught her for a moment, but it turned out to be Ruth, who waved at her from the passenger side as the car parked near the house. An unfamiliar man was driving.

"Well, well," Ruth said, getting out of the car and carrying a bag to hand to Christine. "We weren't expecting you, Chrissy, that's for sure."

"I know," Christine said, deciding to dispense with an apology. After last night, she felt the need to be more assertive. She didn't need to apologize for deciding to stay on her own property, any time she wanted.

"Welcome," Ruth said, "I brought lunch."

"Thank you very much," Christine said, eyeing the driver.

"For gosh sakes, Joey," Ruth called to him. "Come out and say hello to Chrissy."

"That's Joey?" Christine said at the sight of the hulking twenty-five-year-old. "Last time I saw him he was about as tall as you, Ruthie."

Joey was Ruth's son from her first marriage. Five years old at the time of Ruth's divorce, Joey lived full time with Ruth and Ted. Though Joey was born late in Ruth's twenty-year marriage, his arrival probably contributed to the marriage's downfall. Her father had talked about Ruth's sullen son many times, wondering whether Ted might have been better off without her. Even though she'd been good comfort for the widower, the stress brought on by Joey undid most of it.

Joey stood slope-shouldered, looking straight at Christine, saying nothing, his eyes red and probably hung-over. Christine had never met his father, but knew of him. Everyone in Lucid knew Harley Dunn, one of the town's ne'er-do-wells. He'd wound up time and again in jail for an escalating string of offenses. Christine wasn't sure whether the guy was in or out of jail at the moment, but she knew from experience, most likely, and sadly, it was the former. So far, Ted's influence had somehow kept Joey out of trouble with the law.

"Joey was out a little late last night with his friends. You know how it is in Lucid. Especially in the summer. Young people. I don't know where they get their energy."

"Been awhile, Joey." Christine held out a friendly hand, but Joey was either too hung-over or arrogant to take it. He wandered off to the pole barn without comment, the open door the only invitation he seemed to need. She wondered how late he'd been out. And where.

"Joey," Ruth scolded, to no avail. "Kids," she clicked by way of apology to Christine. "Let me help you get these things inside."

"I am starving," Christine said, "and haven't had a moment to grocery shop, so I appreciate it."

"Well, there's enough in here to keep you for a few days." Ruth walked inside her house in a familiar way, and began storing items away in cupboards and the refrigerator.

"Oh," she said, surprised to find dishes stored in the first cabinet she opened. "I see things have been reorganized. Probably by that geologist. Well, let me take care of that for you,"

"No," Christine said, a little more firmly than she had planned. "I mean, it's fine, Ruth. I reorganized things."

"Oh?"

"Really," she said a bit calmer, stopping short of apologizing. "I know, it's probably a bad habit. I wanted the cupboards the way I have them back home." She tried laughing at herself to lighten up the environment. "I'm getting too old to retrain myself, I guess. Don't worry about it. I'll put things away in a bit. But I can't thank you enough, again, for bringing me something to eat. I thought I saw some of your famous icebox cookies packed in there."

"Yes," Ruth said, removing a small package from the bag. "Both Ted's and your dad's favorites." She offered one to Christine and had one herself.

"Now, where are my manners? Would you like a cup of coffee?" Much as she might like to have a word or two with Ruth, she was wondering what Joey was up to in the pole barn. And the security company was due to arrive soon.

"Oh, well I wouldn't want to bother you." She looked at the stove, "And I see you don't have the percolator out."

"Oh, I had completely forgotten about that old thing. In fact, it hasn't turned up yet in my cupboard rearranging." She pointed to the expensive single-cup brewer, "Honestly I can get you one in a minute."

"Well, I'm glad you brought your own," Ruth said, reddening. "Now I remember what happened to it. I . . . I mean . . . Ted and I borrowed it when ours went on the fritz."

"Borrowed it?" Christine said, popping a small pod into her machine and pressing the brew button.

"Oh, we meant to get it right back here. But then that geologist was in here forever."

Which meant, Christine quickly calculated as she got a clean cup out of the cupboard, that they had 'borrowed' the pot last summer. They'd had it an entire year. She stopped herself from asking if Ruth had ever planned to return it.

"Oh, well, that explains it," Christine said, wondering if her cheery tone sounded as irritated to Ruth as it did to her. "But you can see I don't need it. Just go ahead and keep it." She was being a brat. Ted and Ruth had done so much in managing the place in her many years of absence. She owed them more than a coffee pot.

She handed Ruth her cup of coffee and quickly brewed up another.

"There's a sandwich or two in there," Ruth said. "I hope you don't mind I made one for myself, thinking we'd sit and chat a bit."

Christine did, actually mind, but thought she might be overreacting. Ruthie was only doing what small town women always did. Bringing on the welcome wagon. Though Christine was smart enough to know it wasn't just hospitality that had Ruthie out so soon. She was gathering gossip to share with everyone back in town.

"What about Joey?" Christine said, trying to catch a glimpse of him out the window.

Ruth laughed. "He already ate two of them on the way out here. I had to get the bag away from him before he ate the rest."

"I guess I can't say I'm surprised. He's tripled in size since I saw him last." Christine said. "Meaning . . ." she added hastily "he's all grown up. The last time I saw him he was still a kid."

"Oh, he's probably quadrupled in size," Ruthie said. She wasn't a tiny woman herself and the boy's father, Harley, was, as Christine recalled, a giant of a man.

"Let's have our lunch out in the screen porch," Christine said. "You head out there. I'll bring the sandwiches out."

She met Ruth in the screen porch and before the two women had even exchanged another sentence, they watched as Joey ambled out from the depths of the pole barn carrying two oversized coolers and a couple of lawn chairs. He brought them to Ruth's car, popped open the trunk, and set them inside.

"Um, Ruth? Can you tell me why Joey is walking off with things from my dad's . . . I mean, *my* pole barn?"

"Oh. Well. We stored a few things in there," Ruth said between bites, and without any sense of remorse. "Ted thought it would be fine."

The coolers and the lawn chairs looked vaguely familiar. She wondered whether they really did belong to Ruth or Joey. But it been so many years since she'd spent time at her dad's that the story may well have been true. And why wouldn't they borrow some space in the pole barn?

"That isn't a problem, is it? There's plenty of space out there. And no one else has used it since, well, your dad died." Ruth set down her sandwich plate.

First the coffee pot, now space in her pole barn. Last night's intrusion had clearly gotten to Christine. She hadn't even mentioned that to anyone yet. Then of course something even more significant than a coffee pot and space in the pole barn had gone missing. People seemed even less worked up about the fact that an actual person was gone.

Had Joey not accompanied his mother out to the house, she might have thought of bringing up the intruders to Ruth. It was possible that some random person had gotten lost and turned around in her driveway. Or some overgrown teenagers like Joey and his friends were out causing trouble, not expecting to find anyone at the house. Was her mind going overboard?

"I'm..." she almost said it again, but stopped herself short of saying she was sorry if she sounded suspicious. "Of course not. Not a problem. Let's just say that adjusting to life out here is coming a little slow, and leave it at that."

A white box truck began to make its way up the driveway, the business name clearly visible from a quarter mile away.

"Pelican Falls Home Security?" Ruth said. "Is this for real? Boy, you really do jump to conclusions, don't you? Are the police far behind? Ready to haul me off for not returning your coffee pot?"

"Ruth, it's nothing of the sort." Christine wondered if she'd already gone too far. Still, she found it odd that Ruthie seemed to be exaggerating. Why would she think Christine was ready to have her slapped in handcuffs?

Joey stood bowlegged, his beefy arms jutting out, watching as two uniformed men stepped out of the box truck. The two men walked up to him and had a brief conversation. Then he pointed out Christine to them.

He escorted the men to the screen porch.

"Ms. Ivory?" one said. "We're here to install the security system you ordered," the man began, referring to the clipboard he was carrying. "Will you review this order, then initial it to show that you've agreed to have us go ahead with the installation?"

Ruth read over Christine's shoulder, while Joey stood close by, his mouth hanging open.

"Infrared motion detectors? High decibel alarms? What on earth?" Ruth said.

"Let's discuss this order outside," Christine said to the security company employees. She didn't want Ruth broadcasting the exact specifications of her system to Joey, and eventually everyone in town.

As she walked the men around the property, she learned exactly where devices would be placed, both inside of and outside of the buildings. In the next half-hour, she approved the order while Joey and his mother kept watch from inside her house. She asked the men if they could hold off for a few minutes until her company left. She knew her suspicions might be going overboard, but she didn't want to take any chances her security system details would be broadcast with the rest of the gossip about her. She hadn't gotten the friendliest welcome from Lucid, and until she was sure exactly who was on her side, she wanted to have the advantage of being the only one who knew the specifics about her security system.

She trotted back to the screen porch while the men began to set up their workstation in the pole barn.

"I'm really sorry," she said, apologizing for the only time that day. "They require that only the owner be present during installation. We'll have to cut our visit short for today."

"Why on earth are you having such an elaborate system installed?" Ruth said as Christine escorted them back to their car. "Ted won't believe it when I tell him what's going on out here."

Joey gave her a scowl.

Christine knew enough to not confirm exactly how elaborate her system was.

"Just chalk it up to my city nerves," she said. "And a long experience working closely with law enforcement. I'm just used to being surrounded by lots of security, I guess. I had to pass through metal detectors each day on my way to the office. I guess you get used to what you get used to." She considered mentioning the missing geologist, who had disappeared at the end of his stay in Lucid, but someone else made a surprisingly articulate comment in regard to him.

"I guess it isn't exactly comforting to think that the last person who stayed out here is missing and presumed dead," Joey said.

Christine felt her ire rising.

"Joey! You'll scare Chrissy with that story. No one's exactly coming out and saying the guy's dead," Ruth said. "Gosh sakes. Chrissy is going to think we're all murderers out here." Ruth gave Christine a curious glance, before turning back to her son.

"Well. Six months has come and gone without the guy turning up. Doesn't that make him as good as dead?" Joey pointed out, running a finger under his nose, and loudly spitting next to Christine's feet. "And to think, Ted was the last one who saw him alive." He started laughing. "Mom, doesn't that make him the prime suspect in the guy's disappearance. A cop, no less?"

Christine couldn't keep up with Joey's rapid-fire accusations. Why was he pointing a finger at Ted? As far as anyone knew, Adams could have driven back to West Virginia and gotten lost in a storm in the mountains. Still, Joey was right. Ted was apparently the last person who had seen Adams.

"Chrissy would know better than us what makes a person a suspect in someone's disappearance," Ruth said, far more gossipy and much less fearful for Ted then Christine would have expected.

"Goodness," Ruth added. "With these security people wiring up the place and Joey blabbing about murder, you'd think Lucid was the crime capital of Minnesota. I wonder what Joanie would have to say about all of this," she said, shaking her head.

"Mom, your bridge partner says a lot about everything, all of it wrong. She's probably telling everyone that Chrissy's going to open up a yoga clinic out here, just like they have back in the city, and she'll have everyone chanting new age mantras and waving incense around us. Before you know it, we'll have city people coming up here all the time." Joey got in the driver's seat of their car.

"Cults? Good heavens, Joey. Where do you get these crazy ideas of yours?" Ruthie got into the passenger side, then looked back at Christine. "You're not going to start a cult are you, Chrissy? Really that's what you do in the city?"

Christine barely knew where to begin, but before she could even open her mouth to remind them she was a social worker for Mendota County, Ruthie had already moved on.

"Oh, Ted's coming out later with those cats. He wanted to have the vet check them out first for you. He says you're a—what was it—germaphobe. Or something. Wants to make sure the cats are good and healthy enough for you."

"Fine," Christine said. "Whatever." She began walking away from them. Everyone thought she was a germaphobe opening up a yoga cult. What was the point in even trying to talk to these people, let alone get them to focus on serious business? Like finding a missing geologist. Putting to rest all of these rumors about oil.

When they finally drove away, she told the home security people they could start installing her equipment. They promised to have her hooked up and ready to go that evening, which she knew would be soon enough and help keep trespassers out, but do nothing at all for a possibly more insidious problem: the choking gossip spread by the town's grapevine. That the people closest to her were likely instigating the gossip was even worse. Even though Ruth and Ted had never married, they were as good as married given their long time together. That brutish lump of a man-child, Joey, was as close as she would have to a cousin. Neither Joey nor his mother were interested in correcting her story, and instead were spreading rumors about her, and there was nothing she'd be able to do to stop it. And no such thing as a gossip motion detector to alert the proper authorities and clamp down the correct version of her life.

Everyone in Lucid was connected, related in one way or another. And tight knit communities like Lucid used the grapevine to keep family in line and different perspectives out. In less than a day, her real life had been taken over by the version the town created for her—that she was a spoiled outsider set on destroying their small town values and laying claim to the potential riches buried in the ground under Lucid.

Who knew where the story would head next? Maybe the only solution was to put her place up for sale, sell it as fast as she could, and get the hell out of town? It was already obvious that everyone wanted that.

Cutting her connection with Lucid, forever, would mean ending her last ties to her father, the life they had shared on school vacations and summers. That was the last thing she wanted, though, clearly, she wasn't sure she could take much more of Lucid's scrutiny. She wondered what—or who—was going to accost her next.

6

"They are pretty cute," Christine said as the second kitten climbed out of the box Ted set down in her living room, "but honestly, I'm not sure how long I'm going to stay here. And I can't take them back to the city with me."

"Unbelievable," Ted said. "You just got a whole security system wired up out there, you've already got this place looking better than it has in years, and you're still planning on leaving? Yesterday you told me you weren't even sure you wanted to sell this place yet. What gives, Chrissy?"

"I don't know. I wish I knew." A kitten sniffed Christine's outstretched hand, then nuzzled against her knuckles. Without warning, it sunk its pin-sharp claws into her. The other came by, curious to see what trouble it could cause, and instead got batted by its sibling.

Christine didn't flinch. She was already in enough hot water with Ted as it was, and didn't want to possibly offend him by complaining. Besides they were kittens and kittens had claws. She'd had worse run-ins with her human patients. Even the youngest ones had done some real damage, including a five-year-old who had bitten her hard a few years back, sending her to the emergency room for twenty stitches, and leaving a still-visible scar on her hand. That instinct of self-defense was a good sign, even when it caused her pain. It meant that the vulnerable individual (whether that was a young crime victim or a tiny kitten) still possessed a fighting spirit. She was always more concerned about her patients who weren't willing to defend themselves. The ones who'd given up hope.

"I'm going to get the rest of their stuff from the truck," Ted said. "You already told me you don't want mousetraps and you don't want poison. These cats are staying with you for as long as you're here. I don't care if it's a day or the rest of the summer. I'm not taking them back to Ruthie."

She was stunned by the level of outrage he'd expressed, though, being Ted, and a mirror of her father, he'd expressed it just like her dad would have. At about the level of a whisper. How he'd managed to keep a lid on Joey wasn't apparent. But then maybe he hadn't entirely kept him under control, given the fact that Joey might have been the mysterious and unwanted visitor at the end of her driveway the night before.

"Fine," she said. "They can stay." She heard her father's voice in the back on her head, gently reminding her of some words she didn't use often enough.

"Thank you," she said, meaning it.

Ted let the words sink in. "Good. Now, I'm headed back to town to pick up a few more things for you. More cat litter. More cat food. Ruthie pushed me out the door with these so fast I didn't have time."

"I still have so much to do," she began to complain, thinking of how cat litter was bound to get sprinkled across her just cleaned floors.

"I'm pretty sure you don't. This place looks immaculate. I'm telling you to sit down and enjoy your new companions. Geez, you think you'd notice how crazy you got being out here by yourself last night. The tale Ruthie—and Joey—told me when they got back from visiting you this afternoon. Crap. I thought my Chrissy had been replace by, oh, I don't know, a Zombie from one of Joey's horror movies."

She knew better than to object further. If he was anything like her father, he wouldn't leave the house until he saw her doing exactly what he told her. So she sat down on her perfectly cleaned kitchen floor.

"By the time I get back, I want both of them named," he commanded. He waited for her to respond.

"Okay. Names," she mumbled, watching the pair of kittens as they began to investigate her kitchen. They were older than she expected, which was good. She wasn't sure she could have handled a pair of just-weaned kittens. Her father had always kept cats on the property to control the mouse populations, so she knew how to handle and care for them. But it had been years since she'd taken care of a pet. She didn't even own so much as a houseplant in her condo in the city. It was too much work keeping the leaves dusted, the proper amount of water and fertilizer. The right kind and amount of indirect light. Ugh. Such responsibility.

Ted left her there on the floor, seeing her apparently occupied with kittens, not knowing how much she was already starting to obsess over them. But he must have guessed.

"Remember," he said. "Focus. I want names when I return."

"Names, right. Got it." She was barely sure she could take care of the little fuzzballs. Names? Well the man told her to get cracking. Of course she immediately did the opposite. She obsessed more. She hated being responsible for keeping something alive. Cats. Plants. Relationships. It didn't matter what it was, as long as something needed a certain amount of attention, she was sure to go follow the same pattern: apply herself 150 percent, wear herself out with worry that she wasn't applying herself 150 percent, require constant reassurance that she was indeed performing well on the task, in fact superbly, eventually burn herself out (as no one can keep up a 150 percent effort for an extended period of time), then back far, far away, retreating twice as many steps in the opposite direction.

One thing was sure. No one would be giving her a report card on her cat care. School and work had, at least, an external measure that would give her, at least for moments, some measure of what her efforts were yielding. She'd have to rely on purrs for that, with her feline supervisors.

She watched as one kitten investigated a tiny speck of dust that had somehow escaped Christine's thorough dusting. With the one remaining speck of dust occupied by the black kitten, that left the tabby with only one other plaything. Its sister. She hunted and pounced immediately, causing the black kitten to go skittering off in the opposite direction. Almost immediately, the tabby found something else of interest: a broom and dustpan, tucked between the counter and the stove.

"Come on out from there, precious," she said, gently taking hold of the kitten by the scruff of its neck, but it immediately scrambled back into the tight space. Perhaps it was already on the trail of a mouse, hidden back in the corner.

As she watched the kittens playing in her kitchen, she gave the last few months another of many of the reviews she'd done of her most recent job history. She was, she knew, her toughest critic and worst enemy. Indeed, she had lasted a long time in the pressure cooker known as the Mendota County Social Services department.

Her OCD had only gone into high gear at the end, as the habits that had powered her unusual level of hyper-organized productivity at work included the quirky application to organizing her work wardrobe. It had started with her planning out her work wardrobe a week in advance, and ended in an obsessive system to coordinate, plan and label a month's worth of outfits at a time, down to her hosiery and jewelry. She'd detailed the wardrobe plan by labeling hangers by the date the outfit would be worn. The crowning touch—her signature—was coordinating a matching hair color and style.

One month it might be a vibrant shade of red with a splash of platinum blond at the nape of her neck. The next month she might coordinate her plan to go with a jet-black updo, accented with narrow, silver dreads that swam down her neck like tiny snakes. That month someone nicknamed her Medusa, after the classical Greek protectress who had snakes for hair and could turn her enemies to stone the moment they looked at her. She didn't mind being feared, but she didn't care to be made fun of, and the Medusa nickname stuck to her longer than the hairstyle did. For a long time, she hadn't cared that her obsessive planning made her "borderline" on many of the personality disorder tests she gave her patients. This obsession with clothing organization hadn't controlled her life. Nothing controlled her life.

In the end she wasn't so sure. That was when she shaved her hair down to near-regulation Marine length and quit her job.

One of the kittens made its way into her living room, the other ran after it, and Christine, told to stay with them, crawled on hands and knees into her own living room. There she lay on her back, sinking into the rag rug she'd washed that morning. Unexpectedly, it felt more comfortable to her than the bed had felt the previous night, but she really hadn't slept well. She stared at the ceiling, remembering how her organization obsession had begun to swallow her just as her work life began to spin out of control. Her first attempt to counteract it showed up, as would be expected, in her hairstyle: she'd buzzed it off herself late one night, and dyed it an outraged, bruised purple. She began to turn up in the office wearing the same oversized plain black polyester pantsuit for days on end. She seemed to be swimming in the outfit, but the fact was that she was losing weight she didn't need to lose, working late to rewrite case-notes that were already perfect and didn't need to be written. The past spring, she'd turned in her notice to almost no one's surprise. Except perhaps Arvo.

One kitten climbed on top of her, walking along her leg and torso until it found a comfortable spot to curl up between her shoulder and her neck. The other followed its sibling's path, and settled down lightly on her breastbone, purring there until it fell asleep, like its sister. Pinned there under the featherweight of two sleeping kittens, Christine continued to evaluate the madness of the past several months. She tried to figure out when the excitement of planning her wardrobe and her life had turned into a controlling obsession. She knew that this was the one thing that had perhaps drawn Arvo and her together, their habit of avoiding real problems in their lives and instead spending time pursuing the exciting shiny distractions: in her case, a flashy new dress, in his a flashy ex-wife—something, anything, to dress up or cover up or just basically ignore what was really wrong. Finally the day comes when you hit bottom. For her it was the day she dyed her hair purple. For Arvo, maybe it was her telling him it was over. Though she didn't truly believe she could have that much influence. After all, he'd quickly moved on. She just moved away. Were they both still just running away from their problems?

Only a few months had passed since she bottomed out, quit her job, and worked out an arrangement to have the summer off to recharge. She needed to look after only herself. Certainly not these two precious kittens that had curled up contentedly on top of her, and purred themselves to sleep.

Well now she was really stuck. The kittens had fallen asleep and she couldn't possibly move or do anything until they woke up. She'd remembered that silly rule of her dad's, which he conveniently invoked right before dinner needed to be prepared on a summer night. He'd plopped himself down on the couch in the side room, tapping his fingers on his chest to draw the current cat's interest, then quickly claimed he would be unavailable to help get dinner together.

Christine didn't mind, really, getting a meal together for the two of them. While he and the cat took their pre-dinner snooze, she boiled pasta, or scrambled some eggs. Just as conveniently, the cat leapt off him moments before dinner was served.

A sleepy smile spread on Christine's face. The clean rug was so comfortable. The clean room in her father's house so inviting. The kittens were purring away in their kitten dreams. Moments later, there were three asleep on the floor. Christine and her newly named kittens: Precious (the gray tabby) and Semi-Precious (the black one).

7

"Wow," Christine said, yawning and rubbing her eyes. "How long have you been here?"

"Oh, I don't know. An hour?" Ted stood outside Christine's screen door, watching her as she rose from her living room floor.

She opened her door and joined him on the porch, careful to leave the kittens inside.

"You seemed pretty comfortable in there with your new friends," he said.

"I'm surprised to admit it, but we made friends pretty fast." She sat next to him, looking out across the countryside, still drowsy from her nap. Her naptime dreams ebbed way to the landscape, which undulated around them with its own dreamlike stories of the past.

"Just sitting here in this chair, next to you, brings back a lot of memories of my dad," Christine said.

Ted quietly listened.

"Most of them good ones," she said. "I can't remember how many times he drilled all the geological history of this area into my head."

She glanced across the fields to see the boulders he'd pointed out to her, the contours of the glacier-shaped landscape, and memories of how excited he was about all of it.

"Of course, back then I was a complete brat about it." She didn't want to tell Ted how many regrets she'd had about her peevish behavior. How she wished she'd showed she cared more often then. "Now I'm seeing things the way he did. That it is interesting to think about."

"You, Chrissy? Caring about rocks after all these years?"

"I know. Dad would be astonished."

The kittens' sharp complaints finally got their attention. They went inside and Christine announced their names proudly. Ted said nothing and sat at her kitchen table. She noticed he'd seemed unusually quiet since his return. Even for an unusually quiet guy. She asked him again what he'd thought of her response to the order he'd given her before leaving earlier.

"Do you approve?"

A kitten climbed on his lap and he scratched behind its ear absentmindedly.

"I was trying to avoid getting them all riled up," he said, apologizing, "but they only seemed to get more frantic, once they woke up and saw I was outside. So sorry we woke you, you looked like you could use some rest."

She noticed he'd laid aside a newspaper folded open to the crossword section, one that he'd practically finished. "Well," she said, "judging by how far along the crossword is I've been asleep for quite some time. I do feel better."

Now he was the one who was oblivious to others around her. That was the Ted she remembered. She'd always considered him a thoughtful person, an odd fit for a job that required so much interaction with people. But that personality of his was what made him good at his job. He held back his judgment. He was the most patient of listeners. People had counted on him not only to keep the peace, but be the arbiter when domestic battles got of hand.

He'd talked raging drunks out of their houses, preventing spousal violence. He'd talked suicidal farmers into giving themselves a second chance, another growing season to right things, belief that things could be better. He'd talked young runaways back home, or into treatment when drugs sent them spiraling out of control. From stories relayed through her dad, the man sounded like a guy who never stopped talking. That was his best law enforcement weapon, far better than a loaded gun. He'd peppered potential criminals with a quiet wit, a friendly word, and patient and unending willingness to listen to whatever they wanted to unload.

Now retired, he'd become stone quiet. Perhaps after all that time, he'd talked himself out.

"Did you say something?" he said. The kitten scrambled off of him, running off to chase its sibling to the other side of the room.

"Precious and Semi-Precious. Their names. You told me I needed to have names for them when you returned." Perhaps he'd become a touch deaf. Senile. She hated the thought.

He laughed. "Perfect names for little rascals." The introspective look, tinged with a bit of moroseness, clung to him.

"What's up?" she finally blurted. "Cat got your tongue?"

He chuckled. "Good one. At least you're joking now," he said. "I hate to spoil your good mood. I got some news before I came back."

"Go for it," she said, faking a smile and hoping he believed it more than she did. She really didn't want any bad news, but hoped what he had to say wasn't that big of a deal.

"I got a call back at the house. From the geologist's wife."

"They found him?" she interrupted. "About time, if you ask me," she said, biting her tongue.

"No. It's not that," he said. "She says she's coming out here." He waited for her reaction.

It was just what she didn't need, Christine thought, though she kept that opinion to herself, not sure how long she could do that. She didn't want any more unexpected, and likely hostile, visitors.

Just then Ted's stomach growled. Perhaps that was the source of some his dour looks. Feeding him would give her a way of keeping herself occupied while she worked through this latest unexpected bump in the Lucid road.

She held out a chair for him and sat him down in front of an empty plate. "It's way past lunch, but I'm guessing you're as starved as I am. Take a seat. You can tell me more while I get lunch ready."

"She said she planned to stay in Lucid for the foreseeable future," Ted told her as she got more dishes out of the cabinet, taking comfort in how organized it all was, even though it was not the way Ruthie would have done it.

"She asked if I'd make arrangements for her to stay at the nearest full-service hotel. Not sure who she thinks I am. The last time I spoke with her, I was a cop. Now I'm some kind of errand boy."

"Hm. Sounds a little high maintenance if you ask me," Christine said, serving Ted some of the potato salad Ruth had dropped off earlier. "I see that look you're giving me—"

"What look?" he said.

"Like I'm the pot calling the kettle black?"

"Well, since you were the first to mention it, Chrissy, you weren't always this way. So 'high maintenance,' like you say." He saw Christine open the refrigerator. "Oh. Is that some of Ruthie's fried chicken? How about a piece?"

She handed him the container of fried chicken and sat down across from him. "You're right," she said. "About the chicken, I mean. I don't exactly accept that I'm high maintenance." She was starving. Apparently Ted was too. After a few more bites of potato salad and chicken, Ted went on.

"Mrs. Adams says she wants to talk to you," he said, then glanced away. "She said she wants to spend lots of time out here."

"Great," Christine said. "Just what I need, more snooping visitors."

"Besides me and Ruthie, who else has been out here? Unless you're including us in that category. We're practically family!"

She was including Ruthie. And Joey. She wasn't ready yet to lump Ted with that pesky group, which included most of Lucid's

500 residents, all of whom had visited her in her dreams as nightmarish peeping Toms.

She knew she'd finally have to admit what happened the previous night. "Of course not. There were a couple of uninvited guests, late last night. Well, I guess more like early this morning."

Ted's face turned quickly to concern.

Dodged that bullet, she thought, sorry to have hurt his feelings but still not sure if he was 100 percent in her corner. At least he looked like he had some sympathy for her.

"Well, it started with raccoons getting in the screen porch. I'd forgotten a bag of that stuff we found rotting in the refrigerator out there—"

"Sorry, Chrissy, we should have been up here months ago taking care of that—" Ted said with a look of guilt on his face. "—cleaned out the refrigerator, at least."

"You are not to blame for any of this. I should have been out here years ago. Not another word about taking any of the blame." She gave him a sympathetic look. "Why don't I make us some coffee before I get into more of this?"

"Sounds fine," he said, not wanting to wait to continue to hear from her. "So raccoons got in? And that's why you got the place wired up like it's Fort Knox?"

"No," Christine said, popping a pod into her coffee maker.

"Oh. Yeah," he said, with a trace of shame. "Ruthie mentioned the missing percolator when she came home. You're sure it's fine that we keep it?"

"Absolutely," Christine said, returning to the table in a flash with a cup of coffee for him. "And no. Raccoons were not the only trespassers here last night. Though I do need your help with the screen repair, if you can let me know who in town does that. I want to hire someone."

"I'd be happy to take care of it for you myself, this afternoon. I think your dad has some extra screen out in the pole barn. The guy has all the tools in the world, too. Except that we may have borrowed a few here and there . . ." he said.

The thought of Joey carting off some of her dad's tools flashed in her mind.

". . . but I'll look into that for you, make sure everything gets back where it belongs," he said. "I know it sounds bad. Like a lot of stuff has gone missing around here . . . including the last known inhabitant," he said ruefully. "Though I can't imagine anyone's going to blame us for it . . ."

"Except maybe Joey, who has already fingered you as a prime suspect," Christine said, with not much of a joke in her voice.

"Yeah, he's been blabbing that to pretty much everyone in town," Ted laughed. "No one takes anything he says seriously. Certainly not anyone in a position to take that kind of talk as an actual accusation, and run with it. I mean, seriously. A long-time cop responsible for something like this?"

She wondered if she should tell him that the implications were more serious then he understood. Joey shouldn't be telling anyone and everyone that his step-dad was responsible for the guy's disappearance. Ted was lucky he hadn't been grilled more by the Carlson County detectives about it, carted off to the county for a thorough interview, and potentially locked up. But—this being Lucid—who knew what exactly had been investigated. And what might be covered up.

Ted went on without showing any more concern about what Joey had apparently been saying for months. "Ruthie didn't say anything about you having uninvited guests out here."

That's because I didn't tell her, Christine thought, but didn't say. *On purpose. Not with Joey lurking in the background.*

"Did more raccoons drop by? Or was that all it boiled down to," Ted asked, "a hungry raccoon family looking for a late night snack?"

"I didn't get around to telling Ruthie about the other trespassers. The human ones. I had cleaned up the mess left by the raccoons, and was heading out to put the stuff in the pole barn when I heard someone running down the driveway, then saw a car's taillights. Whoever it was took off fast and headed north on the County Road."

"That was it? Your trespassers were probably just some kids goofing off. Maybe a guy pulling over to take care of some personal business behind the trees. It was probably nothing, Chrissy. Geez. You sure are suspicious about people."

"You were the one who said life had changed in Lucid. You warned me about people," she said, getting up to put away the lunch things. "Don't you remember that long chat we had outside the Y Not?"

"I'm sorry to put it to you this way, Chrissy. But you don't have a thing to worry about. A couple of kids using the end of your driveway are no more dangerous to you than racccons trying to get into your screen porch," he said. "Your real problem here is the flip side."

"The flip side?" The calm she'd felt after her long nap with the kittens had evaporated away. Was there some danger she wasn't understanding?

"No, see, here's the thing. People are concerned about you."

"Me? Why on earth?"

"I'm sorry to say, but much as they loved your dad, you're pretty much a stranger here. An unknown. Unknown is dangerous to people here, who are used to what they're used to. They like things to stay the way they are. They don't like strangers coming to town and insisting on doing things their way, and not Lucid's way."

"And so I'm like the intruder. The trespasser on their turf," she said bluntly and angrily. "Right?"

He took another sip of his coffee, his eyes hard. Just like her dad's eyes could harden. When he was telling her things she didn't want to hear.

"Yeah. That about sums it up."

"Funny. I didn't see a big keep-out sign posted at the city limits."

"It's not like that. You can change things, you know. Make yourself more welcome here," he said. "You've got a pretty big chip on your shoulder you know—I'm sorry I have to be so blunt about this—but it is for your own good that I'm telling you this. You need to soften up, Chrissy."

Boy, she'd heard that kind of thing in job evaluations before. That she could be a little too pushy. Bordering on arrogant. What they didn't go so far as to say was that she could be a bitch at times. They couldn't go that far since she was more than willing to march to human resources and claim she was a victim of sexism, that is, if a single look from her didn't get her the result she needed. She wouldn't put up with that kind of bullshit in Mendota County, and everyone knew it.

"Oh really," she said, sarcasm intended.

"Yes, really. Catch more flies with sugar than vinegar, if you know what I mean."

"What on earth would I want to do with a lot of flies? People are being ridiculous, if you ask me. Lucid needs to change and join the twenty-first century, if you want my opinion, which is clearly not wanted around here. It's Lucid that needs to be more tolerant towards the outside world."

"No, Chrissy. You're here in our territory. You're the one who needs to work harder to fit in. It's the cold, hard truth. You need to assimilate. Especially if you expect to stick around here longer than a week or so. Say what you will about it, I've learned from years keeping the peace around here. Sometimes it's better to just go along to get along."

Christine remembered why she had spent less and less time in Lucid after her college years came to an end. It wasn't necessarily because of the demands of her career. The more she experienced of cultural differences, and the more she encountered many different types of people in her line of work, particularly with the new Southeast Asian and Mexican immigrant communities springing up all around the city, the less she felt she had in common with her father's people. She'd seen how hard it was for newcomers to fit in to a large metropolitan area. But at least they had the law on their side.

Here, in Lucid, people were trapped, like flies, to their sweet, deluded memories of the past. But, in Ted's words, that was the thing. That was why nothing changed for them. They never moved. They didn't want to grow and learn and get free of the gummy flypaper past. Any evidence that new ways of thinking were possible, was quickly dismissed as unacceptable.

Still, she couldn't bring herself to argue these points with Ted. She'd had the same discussions with her dad, when he started to become stodgy in his viewpoint and ways. He'd returned to his roots, and become a welcomed member of the community. Though he had traveled the world as part of his job, he preferred to live in Lucid, retiring there permanently. He too had urged her to be more tolerant of the community, arguing that it was better for everyone to accept that like the landscape itself, it took a lot to make changes. She couldn't expect to somehow wear down a town's cultural landscape by insisting that her liberal way of thinking was right, and everyone else's conservative values were wrong. She wasn't a glacier, though sometimes, her father had told her, she could be as abrasive and demanding as one. Her last blowout with him on the topic sealed her absence from him, and Lucid, for several years.

"I can see you don't like what I'm telling you. But you need to know the truth about how to survive here. Particularly now that you're deciding what to do with this place, long term."

They took their cups of coffee outside, sitting on the patio with no more talk between them for a while. The kittens scratched at the door and Christine let them outside to enjoy the warm afternoon. The kittens antics distracted them from their irritation with each other.

"So," Christine said at last, after she'd calmed down and observed Ted had as well. But she knew she had to broach the uncomfortable issue that brought him back to her house.

"When is this geologist's wife coming to town? I'm hoping you'll find a comfortably distant hotel for her to park her high-maintenance self." She smiled.

"She said next week."

"So, I have get along with people here for at least another week," she said. "Try to check my own high-maintenance tendencies."

"Yep," Ted said. "It's for the best. From what Steve told me about his wife, she sounds like a force to be reckoned with. Even he found it difficult to live with her, as much as the guy loved her."

"He told you this?" she said, surprised Ted knew so much about the missing man.

"Not in so many words, but a cop learns how to get a lot of information with not a lot said," he said. "You don't always have to come with guns blazing to get answers," he said. "Sometimes it's better to just sit back and listen."

She doubted he had ever fired a shot.

"Though a gun does make a guy open up pretty quick," he said, quickly reading her thoughts, "but I always relied on good community relations to help me get the info I need. That's the way to keep the information pipeline flowing."

"You're right. That's very true," she answered. She knew that he had a point. She'd seen it in practice in Mendota County.

"She's going to want answers," he said. "She already told me she thinks the police force up here is incompetent. Didn't have a problem saying that to the retired police force."

"Oh, does she?" Christine said, trying hard to rein in her sarcasm. Despite her long, and typically warm experience with Ted, she couldn't avoid the feeling that things would have been done differently elsewhere. Given Mrs. Adams's opinion, Christine thought she and the geologist's wife might get along just fine.

"I'm betting you might agree with her, judging by your lack of response. But honest to Pete. There's a lot of country between here and West Virginia. The guy could be anywhere. And believe me, we looked high and low for him."

"I'm sure you did," Christine said, trying to make herself sound convincing. She hadn't been able to hide much from Ted. She still didn't quite believe they'd exhausted all the possibilities. "I never met the guy, like you did. In fact, I didn't even know about him until yesterday, but I have a feeling that he didn't get that far. Not sure why, I guess it's just a hunch."

"So you appear to be in agreement with Mrs. Adams, I see. I guess I can't say I'm too surprised. Not sure how much more it would take to convince you that we know what we're doing up here. Even though this isn't an expensively equipped operation like you might have down in Mendota County, we do know what we're doing."

She decided it was time to try another approach, one she knew she could make sound convincing. "Look. From the beginning, all I've thought is I want to stay out of this missing geologist thing. But it's all going to land in my lap the moment Mrs. Adams comes to town, whether I want that or not. I told you when I got here that I wanted to forget all about my professional life, which includes, as you know, lots of work hand-in-hand with police departments. The last thing I wanted in coming up here was to get involved in an open investigation."

"Yeah. I remember you telling me about that," he said. "I can see that it hasn't been that easy, catching a break. You kind of walked right into it. It's not fair."

"No. It isn't. But now I really don't have a choice. I better get more acquainted with him, what he was doing, where he might have been. The sooner I can have the facts when Mrs. Adams comes a calling, the sooner for everyone—including all the tongues a'waggin' in Lucid— that we can be rid of her." And Lucid could be rid of Christine, though she wasn't going to mention that quite yet. She wondered if Ted suspected what her real plans were.

"See," Ted concluded. "Now you're already coming around to our way of thinking. Keep the lid on things, manage outside influences to avoid causing lots of inside problems. That was quick."

Christine had other reasons for wanting to see very little of Mrs. Adams, as much as it sounded like they might have the same, abrasive personality. She'd reached a decision about what to do with her property that afternoon, and the more she talked with Ted, the clearer it became that it was the right decision, though she wasn't prepared to tell anyone about it yet. It was hard enough making the decision to begin with. She certainly didn't want 500 people on her case about exactly what steps she planned to take. She'd wait until Mrs. Adams had come, gotten her answers, collected her husband's parka, and gone.

After that, the for-sale sign was going up.

8

"THIS SHOULDN'T TAKE LONG," TED SAID to Christine after looking at her torn porch screen. He headed off to the pole-barn to gather the necessary tools, but returned empty-handed not soon after.

"You didn't find anything?" she said, trying hard not to issue an accusation.

He politely waited, holding his empty hand out.

"Oh, right. New keys," she said. "Tell you what, I'll open it for you."

"Wow. You really don't trust anyone, do you? Not even me?"

She paused perhaps a fraction too long. "No. No, you're right. They're in the kitchen drawer next to the sink." The usual place her dad had left them. She considered putting the keys in a new location, but had changed enough of the security for one day, that she relied on the habitual place, if only for that one item. "Help yourself."

He retrieved them and headed off, while she got her kitten supplies situated in her dad's bedroom. She glanced out to the porch and saw Ted had not yet returned to begin his "simple" repair work.

She washed the lunch dishes and swept the kitchen floor, and when she glance towards her porch again, she saw nothing had changed and Ted appeared, a few moments later, once again empty-handed, except for the keys.

"I locked up for you, don't worry," he said, his face red and sweaty. "I was sure there was a roll of screen out there, along with wire snips and the other things a guy would need to fix a torn screen, but doggone it, the stuff's gone," he said, heading out to his truck. She followed and said nothing.

More of her father's belongings had apparently walked away then even Ted knew. The place had been under the town cop's watch, and even he hadn't been able to prevent things from being lifted. She was glad she'd asked the security company to install new locks on all the doors, including the big garage door for the pole barn. Who knew how many people had keys to the place.

"Don't you worry now. I have a hunch where they got to. We had a big storm a few years back," he said, scratching his chin.

A few years back . . . she wondered how many.

"Trees were down everywhere. I remember the plumber's fence got pretty well wiped out, and his wife raises toy poodles. Nasty yappy little things. Anyhow, I remember that he might have drove out here and borrowed a few things. I gave him the key. Poor guy, what a mess. He probably borrowed—"

Borrowed, she thought. *How about downright stole?*

"—borrowed your dad's chainsaw, too. I'll take care of it, come back out in the morning and fix everything up."

He drove off in a hurry. She wasn't sure whether he was hurrying to find her things or hurrying to get away from the irritated owner, as fast as he could. She began to think that she had a far worse problem then the few rodents getting inside her apparently porous property. Had the entire town been out, taking whatever they wanted from the place, with no intention of returning any of it? She made a mental note to add a rather detailed task to her list.

Inventory.

She was going to sit down and inventory every item on the property, and see if she could match things against her father's carefully organized records.

Given what she had learned in the past day, it was likely not going to take time to conduct the inventory. In all likelihood, much was likely gone. But she knew it would be relatively easy to figure out what was missing.

The apple didn't fall far from the tree. She was her father's daughter, each of them fitted with personalities that survived best with order and well-designed organizational systems. He'd been a systems analyst, charged with huge systems installation projects for a multinational data management company headquartered in Minneapolis. By the time he retired, he'd received more than one employee-of-the-year trophy, and earned many bonuses for the quality and timely installation of his systems' projects. Had her father still been living, she had no doubt that he would have had a computerized system to keep track of things in Lucid. But maybe not. He preferred to forget the systems hardware, and do things old school in Lucid. Or not even bother at all. He would say, "busman's holiday," joking about his desire to keep things low-tech in Lucid.

His paper-based system would work just fine for now, as long as the mice hadn't got inside the small file cabinet in his bedroom closet. One of her summer jobs at the house had always been filing, and she invented a system that her father was quite proud of, a carefully curated set of color-coded index cards for various types of household and pole barn items. It came back to her: pink for plumbing, green for electrical, blue for the pole barn, yellow for the house. Numbers and letters were also used. Her dad could know at a glance what might have been lent out (as his was the best stocked pole barn in town), and to whom, though he didn't always keep track of things as well as she did. He would tell her that it wasn't necessary to go overboard in Lucid. People would return things when they got around to it.

She didn't like his loose recordkeeping, and always knew she needed to update his index cards every summer. "Here she comes," he would say, when she arrived by Greyhound bus on summer breaks. "The queen bee of the card index." He knew that she relished putting all of his receipts in order, tracking repair records, buying the office supplies beforehand to upgrade the system each year. He gently took her scolding when she found receipts out of order, improperly filed index cards, loaned items not tracked and correctly filed in the on-loan section of her card index, tools that needed to be replaced because they hadn't been accounted for, and now her father didn't know where they were.

One year she'd added gummed stars to signify if an item was in need of replacement or was missing. Gold for replace, silver for just plain gone. She would immediately send him off to buy replacements for the gold starred items and hassle him all summer about asking around on the silvers. Once the newer replacement was added, the old card for the retiring tool wasn't ever thrown away. She would write up a brand new card, her easy-to-read lettering made in permanent ink the first time, with no mistakes. She delighted in being able to pick up one of his screwdrivers, and recite from memory where and when he purchased it, her memory quickly locating and recalling the index card information, word for word.

Eventually, by the end of summer, he would tire of her pestering him about the silvers. "You can be relentless—" he would eventually say, throwing up his hands, "—to a fault. It isn't pretty."

She would frown, confirming exactly what he'd said, but still awaiting an explanation as to why he hadn't yet found a lost item.

"It's gone," he said. "I don't care." The last thing she wanted to do was to change the star from silver to gold. It bugged her that things were gone, and she was on a mission to have the equipment recovered, only replacing things as a last resort, or when they truly required a replacement.

But it eventually came to that. The last two weeks of summer break involved large purchases at the Pelican Falls Fleet Farm, Christine driving there herself with a handful of index cards with gold stars and her father's credit card. The cheery sight of the well-stocked and perfectly organized aisles at the Fleet Farm did much to eliminate her irritation. The moment she walked through the door, she was greeted by a smiling, helpful sales person who knew exactly where things could be found in the huge Fleet Farm inventory. Her kind of person.

Occasionally an item was no longer carried, and she would have to find a suitable similar item. There were always a few that couldn't be replaced any longer, and no substitute was available. She didn't care if her dad didn't actually use the missing tool anymore. It wasn't right that even one no longer needed tool was gone and she couldn't bring herself to rip up the card and throw it away. She grieved when it came down to filing a card in the MIA section, hoping that one day she'd recover the tool, or find a close-enough replacement. She would take it up the following summer, haunted because she could neither find, nor purchase, the proper replacement. In her most irritated moments, she'd bring out the set of MIA cards and line them up on the kitchen counter like they were tombstones in a cemetery. She mourned the terrible waste of poorly recorded tool loans while gazing at the fallen: her trusty and reliable color-coded index card foot soldiers.

Obviously no recordkeeping had been done in at least ten years, even longer considering that Christine's father had long thought her system over the top. Christine had a week to get the files up to date. She was giving Ted a week to find everything that he knew of that had gone missing, not informing him of the deadline. Then she was going to report the rest of the items as stolen, turning over copies of the applicable receipts, a full accounting of the last known borrower of the item, and a due date for when she expected the police to either fine the culprit or tell her of the location of the missing item.

She didn't, however, expect that the Lucid police department, i.e., whoever had replaced Ted, were likely to help her get things back. Most likely the current cop had a few of her father's tools in his garage. But she had no intention of playing nicey-nice. People had been stealing from her property, and it was time to put an end to it. She was going on record with her grievances with the town. A little voice in the back of her head—that sounded suspiciously like her dad—nagged at her conscience, just like he used to nag at her in person. Telling her really she had no need to take things so far. That it was going to make things more difficult for her, rather than improve the situation. She shut it out, reasoning that if she was going to sell, then she wanted people to pay for what they'd already taken from him. *From her.*

She had another task, far less time consuming, but one she hadn't had the nerve to actually write down. How could she adequately write, in an actionable manner, "Find Someone I Can Trust" on her to-do list?

It was a specific-enough task, but still not terribly defined. One thing clear to her was that no one in Lucid fit the bill. Not even Ted, whom she did consider the one person in town who might have been trustworthy, given his previous job. Still, he had dismissed so many of her concerns already, and was as much to blame as anyone for the missing tools. He'd been well aware of her father's system. Did he think so little of his best friend and his daughter that he dispensed with the necessity to account for their rights as property owners? Granted, Christine hadn't shown any interest in the place until recently, but she thought everyone, even ten years later, might have shown a smidgeon of respect at least for her dad.

So whom could she trust, if she could place absolutely no confidence in Lucid? The Lucid police force, past and present, might have passed along some helpful information, but she didn't have any faith that she would get accurate details on what she needed to know about the missing geologist. Ted had answered defensively, at best. At worst—who knew, maybe he needed to cover his tracks for a poorly executed search, and that was why he dismissed her concerns. His replacement wouldn't have as much to offer, having been hired a few months after the search. The Carlson County Sheriff's office might have information, but it would not be freely shared with her either. She didn't know how close their ties were with Lucid: most likely very close. She expected she'd get the cold shoulder from Pelican Falls.

Once she exhausted her list of potentially trustworthy candidates, which really didn't take very long, as almost everyone in the vicinity could be quickly dismissed. She knew there was really only one alternative. A man she was certain she could trust, but had been determined to never speak to again.

Detective Arvo Thorson of Mendota County.

Even though Arvo might know nothing about the geologist's disappearance, or the investigation, he might be able to get her in touch with people he knew could be trusted in Pelican Falls. She knew it was a long shot. Still, if she could talk to one person and confirm that her hunches weren't crazy—that the investigation hadn't gone as it should have, something, anything that would help her to believe that she wasn't blowing things out of proportion. Ted, Ruth, Joey, and by now everyone in town was convinced her default setting was set to "overreact."

She didn't write the task on her list since it had, in fact, been in the to-do column since before she arrived in Lucid. She was going to screw up the courage to call him, eventually. Despite their failure as a couple, his hang-ups with his ex-wife that always seemed in the way, she had always trusted him. She didn't like his lack of organization. She hated that he never bothered turning up when she had scheduled time for him on her calendar, but barged in when he saw fit. But she had always trusted him.

She'd been forced into learning more about Adams. His wife was coming to her, and she'd be damned if another woman came to Lucid and got the reception she did. She felt she owed the woman something, though she wasn't sure exactly why.

So, it had been decided. Arvo would be consulted. And it would have to be after normal business hours. She didn't want to talk to or be forwarded to anyone else in Mendota County. His cell phone number was still in the speed-dial directory of her phone. His number hadn't drifted too far down on her recent caller list. She hated to admit it, but she didn't like him dropping below the cut line, and, even worse, off the list of her most recent 10 callers. The unfamiliar face of Lucid was too unwelcoming. She needed a dose of her old life, even though parts of it had driven her nuts. She wasn't sure what Arvo might think of her suddenly calling him, but because she was calling on somewhat professional business, she thought it might help justify contact between the two of them.

She certainly couldn't call him up for merely personal reasons.

She set her cell phone on the kitchen table after she returned from a trip to a neighboring town, where she picked up a week's supply of groceries, completely avoiding Lucid's small, adequate grocery store. At the moment, she wouldn't be caught dead in town. She knew the next few weeks were going to be a siege, and she wanted to be well-supplied. After putting the groceries away, she went about her business in the house and pole barn for the remainder of the day, starting her inventorying, and occasionally being forced, by the presence of a lap-requiring kitten or two, to take a badly needed break. Every time she passed by the kitchen table, she stared at the phone, knowing the time would come, late in the evening, when she'd pick it up and dial the fifth number on her recently called number list.

It was past sunset when that time finally arrived. Christine had just switched on the security system. She'd brought the kittens inside for the night, confining them to her father's bedroom while they got used to their new environment, and while she got used to having cats underfoot again. She found a citrine candle or two in a kitchen cupboard and carried them out to the screen porch, lighting them to ward off the mosquitoes that were now able to enter through the raccoon door.

The last thing she did was to get the bottle of Jim Beam down and carry it out to the screen porch, along with a small crystal shot glass. She was going to settle down and talk on the phone with an old acquaintance, one she had once considered a friend, a man who had been her lover briefly, but significantly.

She scrolled down her list of recent callers, hit dial, and took another sip of Jim Beam while she waited for him to answer.

9

CHRISTINE WAS ANSWERED IMMEDIATELY BY Arvo Thorson's voicemail greeting. The sound of Arvo's voice, even the recorded one, hit her hard. The authoritative but somewhat worn-down message was pleasingly familiar, but the fact that he was not immediately available by phone, and so many miles away, brought her unexpectedly near tears. Crap. She did miss him more than she would admit to anyone.

She scrubbed her eyes and rationalized anyway. It had been hell. A familiar voice, even her mother's, might have the same effect. It was close to ten o'clock, she wasn't sure why she expected him to answer right away. *Damn*, she thought while wracking her brain for a suitable message to leave. Why hadn't she prepared for this possibility? The phone slipped out of her hand, clattering onto the screen porch deck under the table next to her. She fell to her hands and knees, reaching under the screen porch table in the dark frantically trying to find it.

The first thing she found was a sliver. She could hear the greeting was nearing its end, the beep announcing itself, then the pause that awaited her message.

She grabbed her phone and was almost ready to hit the hang-up button when she remembered that her number would turn up as a missed call, so she would have to suck it up and say something.

"Hey, Arvo," she began, slightly out of breath. "It's me. Christine." She panted a couple of times more, and Arvo's phone disconnected during her pause.

"God damn," she swore. Now she'd have to call back and leave another message. She sat down, and got her breathing under control, the splinter out of her finger. She poured another shot of Jim Beam.

Then her phone rang.

It was Arvo.

She felt both panicked and relieved. She let it ring a second time while she took another sip of the Jim Beam.

"Hello?" she said.

"Christine, it's me, Arvo." His voice sounded distant, but strong. He'd been recovering from a gunshot injury from the last case they'd worked on together and had a collapsed lung as well. The last time she had spoken with him, he had difficulty breathing and talking at the same time. Now he sounded almost normal. Better than normal.

"Oh, of course," she said faking a light tone. But she knew it sounded asinine.

"You called? I'm not sure if you left a message or not, I haven't checked yet," he said.

"Well, I, uh, didn't leave much of a message. I got cut off."

"Oh," he said. "I wonder if my phone is having reception problems. Or something."

"Um, no, it was probably my fault. Actually I'm pretty sure it was my fault. Look, I . . ." she realized the phone call was not at all going as she planned. She shifted back to her script. "Am I bothering you or anything? Sorry, I should have asked that right away."

"Not at all. In fact, I'm on vacation."

"Wow, you. On vacation." She stammered. "Then I am bothering you. Since you're on vacation."

"Oh. Not at all. Actually, I meant we—Jade and I—you remember her. The artist? We're up along Lake Superior, the North Shore, for a week."

"Nice," she said, thinking how nice it would be if she was on vacation at a neutral location like the beautiful landscape along Lake Superior. Rather than in such hostile territory.

"It's been great. My medical leave is up next Monday, and we thought it was a good time to get away. Jade's art show opens next week, too. You should come see it," he said. She could hear how proud he was of her.

"Well, that might be nice," she said, "But I'm not in Somerset Hills for the next, I don't know, couple of weeks. I'm up at my dad's place."

"Oh. On vacation, too? Your new job didn't start yet, did it?" he said.

She thought he might have known, given that she had gotten her job through a friend of his in another county. But Arvo had obviously had other things on his mind than Christine's professional life.

"I arranged to start in September," she said.

"That's right," he broke in. "I've been kind of out of touch with the department lately," he said.

"You sound better," she said, remembering how close he had been to death, given the graveness of his wounds. "You sound good."

"So what are you doing out in Lucid, if it's not vacation?" he said.

"I have some business to take care of at my dad's place, and it seemed like a good time to take a break. On a vacation from work, that's for sure. But not much else. You can imagine how hard it is for me to relax, anyway."

"Yeah. Kind of unusual for both of us. I can't remember the last time I took a vacation," Arvo said.

"Well, you sound healthy," she said. "Strong. Vacation suits you." She sipped the last of her Jim Beam, but still felt edgy. She unlocked the screen porch and stepped outside to the patio, breathing deeply the cool evening air. She immediately noticed how stars brightened the pitch-dark country sky. There were so many more visible than in the city, where she could rarely see more than the Big Dipper and a few bright planets.

There were so many visible stars that it was impossible to shape constellations from the confused jumble of bright, twinkling lights, many of which were clustered so tightly together it was hard to distinguish where one star ended and the next began. Even the Milky Way was more like a long, dazzling stellar superhighway than an indistinct smudge. The country night sky was like her life at the moment: very little clarity in a field of so much competing energy.

"Thanks," he said. "I think I'm almost back to one-hundred percent." He cleared his throat.

She apologized again. "Look, I shouldn't be bothering you. On your vacation."

"Really, it is no bother. It sounds like—you need something? From me?" he said. "Are you all right?"

She said, "I'm fine," but her voice broke. Clearly she was not fine.

"Must be tough to be at your dad's place, I would imagine. Been ten years now, hasn't it?" Arvo picked up on the cues.

Arvo had, in fact, come to her father's funeral, surprising Christine with his unexpected appearance. He'd still been married then, but he came to Lucid alone, delivering a check to the Lucid War Veteran's Memorial, on Mendota County's behalf. Arvo's dad had been a Korean War vet, just like Christine's, and he told her he was honored to be there in memory of both of their fathers.

"Ah. Yes," she said, biting back tears. "It helps that they've thrown out the welcome mat for me this time around. Held a parade in my honor."

"I see," he said.

The pause told her that he immediately understood that the opposite had been the case.

"Ivory, you can take it," he said. "They'll come around to your way of thinking."

"Right. Just like you did."

He laughed. "Maybe I can offer them expert advice in how to get along with you."

"No one knows better than you," she said, "how to tolerate my whacko tendencies." Now she laughed. She told him about her elaborate indexing system, and the reception she expected it would receive. She admitted it might be a little over the top.

"A little?" Arvo said. "Sounds like classic Ivory to me. Have you thought of maybe . . . um . . . going a little easy on folks? Since you're new in town?"

Even though she was starting to see how she might be taking things a bit far, she couldn't help but point out that, really, people were getting away with outright theft.

"Your dad wouldn't have thought that," Arvo said. "Would he?"

She didn't answer him right away, but couldn't help but ending up agreeing with him. "Oh, probably not."

"But it's the principle of the thing, right? That it messes with your system?" he said.

"Yeah, I guess," she said. "Still—"

"Hogwash, Ivory. You're bothered that everything isn't neatly organized, just like you like it. You haven't used any of that stuff for years and now, well . . ." His voice trailed off. "Maybe it's all part of your grieving process. Who knows. For sure if you came after me with one of those silver stars, it would be as good as pointing a gun at me. I'd hand everything over, and more, just to get off your list."

"Yeah, right, Arvo. You were always so responsive and timely whenever I asked you for anything."

They both laughed.

"Probably you never expected me to say this to you, but, Arvo, hearing your voice is the best thing that's happened to me in days," she said.

"Well then, I can tell that things must be terrible out there if me talking to you is the highlight so far," he told her. "What's going on out there that would cause you to call me, of all people?"

When she was the one who'd cut off their relationship. Told him she was done. Neither of them brought up how significant a break it had been.

"I need your help with something. I really didn't have anywhere else I could turn," she said.

"Well this is even more serious than I thought," he said without laughing this time. "Or you wouldn't be calling me. I'm guessing I'm the last person on your list."

She detected still wounded feelings. "That's just not true. And it's a police issue. Maybe I haven't always thought you had the best judgment, but when the chips are down, and they really are, I know you. And I know I can trust you."

"Well that's nice to hear," he said. "Coming from you. I know you have unusually high standards."

Everyone knew. Some would have said unachievable standards, using words far less politically correct to make it clear exactly what kind of a woman they thought she was with her out-of-touch vision of how the world should work.

"And, well, now that I know you're away from the office, I don't even want to ask you."

"Hm. Well now I'm all ears. What on earth could possibly be getting on the usually ironclad bravado of Christine Ivory? Hang on a sec."

She heard him exchange a few words with Jade, the beautiful artist Arvo had taken up with after Christine told him it was over between them. She'd met Jade at the hospital, and could instantly tell that Jade and Arvo had clicked. Who would have thought the combo of young hip black urban woodcut artist and middle-aged sloppy, stodgy, Scandinavian-Minnesotan would wind up working out. But perhaps that was why it worked. She'd seen some of Jade's woodcuts, how the dark and light lines combined into vibrant, unique textures, harmonious yet distinct. Contrasts could work beautifully, as Jade's artworks proved.

It was so unexpected, so unlike what happened with the combination of Christine and Arvo—they'd grown up in the same town, gone to the same high school, ended up working for various departments in Mendota County: in short they'd had everything in common, including often being coworkers on the same cases. Beyond their common upbringing and work environment, there was chemistry, undeniable chemistry, between them. But together they were caustic acid, rather than a complex, excellent wine.

"Okay, I'm back. Now, start from the beginning. Tell me what's going on. Don't leave anything out," he said. "Jade has just handed me a big old boat of red wine. She got the sense this is going to take some time, and told me to be sure to take all the time I needed."

"She's a special woman," Christine told him, meaning every word.

So she started from the beginning, going back over the strange and disturbing experience of coming to what should really be an adopted hometown for her. She relayed none of her suspicions, only trying to give him all the facts, unfiltered through her opinions or feelings. Arvo keyed in on exactly the concerns that had been bothering her, putting into words what she'd been thinking. He agreed with her impression that, given the hysteria regarding the oil issue, and the famous geologist's disappearance, he'd have expected there would be much more interest in locating the guy. Christine told him she hadn't seen any law enforcement bulletins—nor so much as a poster tacked to a telephone pole—that Adams was missing and any information citizens might have about his whereabouts should be reported immediately.

"Did anyone mention whether the property had been searched? Did anyone come to you at any time over the past six months with a search warrant? I find it incredible that some of the guy's possessions were still at your house. Those should have been immediately collected and taken into evidence."

He articulated rapidly what appeared to be numerous law enforcement errors. In his judgment. "And your dad's best friend was the town cop at the time?"

"The one and only, and for the past fifty years. He retired this spring. They grew up together here."

"Do you know who the new cop is?"

"Nope. But for all I know, he's related to half the town, friends with the rest, which automatically puts him on my enemy list. It's the first time I've said that. I'm pretty sure everyone hates me."

"Well, we both know," Arvo said, "that you do tend to rub people the wrong way. Even under the best of circumstances, Christine. Let's just be honest."

She knew. It irked her to have him bluntly state that, but they'd long been direct with each other. It was nothing she hadn't heard before. She had hoped to figure out how to change that, maybe get a fresh start in Lucid. That fresh start was coming, pretty rapidly, to a screeching halt.

"Is there some way any of this casework can be checked out?" Christine asked him. "And quietly?"

"I really don't know anyone in that part of the state," Arvo said. "And of course it's clearly outside of my jurisdiction."

"That, and of course, you're on vacation," she said.

"When does a cop ever go 100 percent on vacation?"

"Well they seem to be permanently out to lunch up here," Christine pointed out, "considering the amount of material that's gone missing from my dad's property. I guess the lack of enthusiasm in the enforcement of trespassing laws pretty much sums it up. If it isn't nailed down, and you can carry it away, by all means go ahead. Doesn't matter if it belongs to someone else."

Arvo asked Christine to go over the particulars again, making sure that he had all of the available detail. "Besides the former cop and his family, is there anyone else in town, that you know might be connected to the missing geologist? Anyone to profit, somehow, by his disappearance?"

"I haven't made it a point to check around," she said. "And most of the people I come across give me the cold shoulder. Who knows, maybe everyone in town conspired against him, for whatever reasons they might have had?"

"And no word on his final report? Nothing?"

"Not that anyone is saying. I keep thinking what we would know by know if Kieran had been on this case," she said.

"Yeah," Arvo said. "He's something else. I can still barely operate a cell phone."

They both laughed.

"I'll make some calls," Arvo said as they were nearing the end of their conversation, sometime near 1:00 a.m. Both of their cell phones were drained, their batteries nearly dead. "Sorry if I can't do too much for you over the next couple of days. I'd like to check a few things out in our databases before I start raising suspicions. Whenever I hear about the kind of situation you're experiencing up there, I wonder if internal affairs needs to get involved. But it's not clear if this is a county or local problem yet. And if anyone gets wind of an internal investigation, you can bet things are going to shut down, mighty quick."

"Well, I can't tell you how much better I feel after talking to you tonight, Arvo," she said. "I bet you never thought you'd hear me saying something like that."

"I have a magic effect on women," he joked. "Seems to work on everyone, except for you, usually."

An unspoken moment passed. Christine wondered why it had been so difficult to need him when he was within reach. Why it had been so hard to forgive his momentary lapse. Why she was always so unforgiving.

"I'll get back to you as soon as I can. But, like I said, it's going to be a few days. And I might end up with nothing to tell you.

And, there is a possibility that everything has been thoroughly checked out, and the guy is just plain gone."

"That seems pretty unlikely if my experience at my dad's place is an example of how things get checked out."

"Ivory—let's be clear. I promise you I'll do everything I can to get you information. But from what I'm hearing, you might be a little off base." He was sounding worn down.

"Sounds like good old Arvo to me," she said wearily. "Not wanting to believe that my opinion on a case has as much merit as yours."

"I didn't say that," Arvo said. "Look. You're tired. You haven't had the best welcome up there. You know that you create tension and conflicts. And I do trust your judgment, so don't go off on me. I'm just saying that you can't shut down and decide what's happened, not quite yet. You can't jump to conclusions when neither you, nor I, know what's been done."

She realized that she'd pissed off the only person she could trust. "You're right," she found herself quickly saying. "I'm sorry. You're right."

He said nothing.

"Shocked, aren't you," she pointed out, surprising herself with a weak laugh, "that I told you you're right and apologized—in the same sentence."

"Well, maybe Lucid is doing more for you than you think," he said, "even if you haven't had the best time. Just relax, if you can. Let me check into things. Try and consider it a vacation and lay off waving your index cards at people for a few days."

Just then, her battery finally quit, and the line went dead. She thought of plugging her phone in and calling him right back, just to end the call on a more graceful note. But she knew there was really nothing more to say that hadn't already been said.

She was drained and dragged herself inside the house, making sure that all of the doors and windows were locked. Even though she'd already checked before calling Arvo. She decided that she would try and do what he said. Relax. An almost impossible task for her, something that seemed to come far more easily to him. Of course, he had the influence of a caring woman, one who seemed to be giving him what she never could. Acceptance. Patience. Big bowls of wine.

She fell into a dead sleep the moment her head touched the pillow, not aware that she'd ended up in her dad's bedroom with the kittens.

10

CHRISTINE SURVEYED THE HIGH SHELVES in the pole barn from its dirt floor the next morning, realizing quickly that she had a long day ahead of her, and she couldn't start until she'd located one of several ladders she knew her dad owned. She hoped at least one of them—and a long enough one—wasn't among the MIAs.

She quickly realized she had forgotten about the pre-task tasks: materials that needed to be located so she could start what she actually planned to do. A certain amount of order was required in order to tackle disorder. She swallowed hard.

Suck it up, Ivory, she told herself. She went looking for ladders in the place where she knew her dad had always kept them, near the front of the pole barn, where they could be easily retrieved for any job. The vaulted, cavernous structure was over two stories high, with plenty of space to store boats and farm equipment, including a small tractor and its plowing and mowing attachments. She'd driven the little tractor herself, using it to cut the grass along the driveway and in the small yard during summer. Once, during a Christmas break, she test-drove a nifty little snow-blowing attachment, managing to clear most of the long uneven driveway herself. Christine noted the tractor parked where it belonged, surprisingly.

She wasn't terribly surprised that the ladders were nowhere to be found. She walked through the entire pole barn interior and saw them nowhere. She explored the exterior, finally locating one ladder: an old wooden extension ladder, hung from a couple of rusty hooks on the exterior of the building. She hoped it was serviceable, and long enough to reach the upper shelves.

She hauled the thing inside and extended it to its maximum length, seeing that it was going to require that she stand on the top rung in order to see what was on the highest shelves. Thankfully, she was unafraid of heights, remembering an incident with Arvo when she learned that he wasn't. He'd learned about her lack of fear in that area on that day as well. She put him out of her mind, hoping he was finding out enough about the missing geologist that would allow her to quickly dispatch Mrs. Adams the following week.

She tucked her clipboard under one armpit, stuck a flashlight in the back pocket of her shorts, and climbed the ladder to the top. She had considered starting at the bottom and working her way up, but it seemed somehow more logical to her hyper-organized mind to start at the top and work her way down. Several of the rungs seemed slightly loose in their fittings, but she thought they seemed acceptable to hold a trim woman, but not a Lucid man. Probably that explained why it was still available for use. The better ladders were all in use elsewhere, likely pinched long ago and in various other Lucid households so long that people had forgotten they'd been "borrowed" with every intention of being returned, someday.

"Anyone home?" someone called from outside, startling the dusty silent air of the pole barn.

Good grief, Christine thought. Could she not have a day go by without an unexpected visitor? She headed back down the ladder, nearly falling when one rung slipped under her feet. Then she swore aloud, alerting the stranger as to her whereabouts.

"Well, Chrissy Ivory. What are you trying to do up there: get yourself killed?" The stranger laughed a little too easily at his own remark.

The voice sounded familiar to Christine, but as her visitor was standing just outside the pole barn, and her pupils were set to the level of the dim interior, she couldn't see who it was.

She reached the bottom and set the clipboard down, walking out to see who'd come calling, and too damn early in her opinion.

"Remember me?" the man said, holding out his hand to her. "Greg LaBelle."

The voice clicked, but not the face. She remembered a Greg LaBelle, a man her dad's age. But this guy was younger. She noticed that his nails were nicely manicured, his hands the smooth, uncalloused skin of a guy who didn't work all that hard, but played hard. He had a sportsman's tan and a playboy's grin, and in a moment it registered.

"Junior," he said, belatedly adding this. "Greg LaBelle, senior, is my dad. Or, was my dad. He passed a few years back."

Of course, Christine remembered. She knew both LaBelles, but this younger one standing before her had gained quite a bit of weight from the skinny, hard-muscled kid she remembered from her college days. His father, Lucid's richest man, was very well known. Judging by the size of the heavy gold watch around the younger LaBelle's wrist, his son had taken his inheritance, and doubled, or tripled it.

"Yes," Christine said, accepting his hand, pleased by the fact that hers was already sweaty and dirty. "I remember you and your dad." Greg LaBelle, senior, been another of her father's longtime friends. The men had bonded as boys when both grew up in Lucid. Her father had told her stories about their many days fishing Lucid's lakes, hunting Lucid's forests, and generally getting in trouble in the way boys do.

She remembered that the two might have had a falling-out towards the end of her dad's life, when LaBelle senior kept pushing her dad to sell part of his land to him. Her dad regrettably began to limit his contact with LaBelle, hoping they could mend fences soon. "Can't let a grudge last long around here," he'd said. "You never know when you might need someone. Burning bridges doesn't do anyone a favor."

Christine was uncomfortable with the idea of carrying one generation's quarrel to the next, but she didn't have the same perspective about grudges, and given her plan to inventory all of her dad's stuff and chase down potential suspects to get his things back, she knew there might be a lot of burning bridges to come. Since she was already planning to cut her ties, she had nothing to fear by stoking the flames.

She remembered the son had taken over his father's real estate business: the gigantic billboard just outside of town summed up everything she needed to know. The real LaBelle, junior, was looking at her with the same well-fed face she'd seen on the billboard when she drove into town. And this visit was not likely to be a social one only. Still, she felt obliged, whether she liked it or not, to entertain what he might have dropped by to discuss. Like it or not, she might have to work with LaBelle to sell her dad's place. She wanted to get to know him better before telling him of her plans.

"Can I offer you anything? Coffee?" She was pleased that her voice sounded pleasant: she'd switched instantly into all-business mode. Even though she was not happy to have her plans for the day interrupted, she thought she'd try the approach Ted mentioned and see if it helped get her what she needed.

"Sugar?" she asked a few minutes later, handing LaBelle a cup of freshly brewed coffee.

"Sure," he said, his cell phone buzzing on her kitchen table. He glanced at the just-arrived message, and scrolled through a few more.

"Oh, I see you have the mini-coffee brewmaster? Nice. I have the super-loaded version at my place. You know the one—grinds and brews, automatically froths your cream if you want it, measures out the sugar for you?"

"Of course you do," Christine said, regretting that slip of sarcasm. The sugar approach. "I wish I had that one," she quickly added. "Pardon my envy."

"No problem." His phone buzzed again and he answered yet another message, then set the phone on silent and turned it face down on her table.

"So many modern conveniences, but sometimes it gets irritating, you know?" His enormous hand dwarfed the delicate cup Christine handed him. She could see the tan-line on his wrist at the edge of his watchband.

He licked his lips when she looked up from his wrist, and she shivered in repulsion.

"Oh, yes," Christine said lightly, returning to her coffeemaker to avoid making eye contact while she finished brewing a cup for herself. "That's why it's nice to get away from it all." She made a show of walking to the windows that looked out on the wide expanse of her land around her. "Shall we go outside? It's looking like a beautiful day."

"Certainly," LaBelle said.

The guy's presence inside her house was unnerving, the scent of his cologne so powerful that Christine was nearly choking. But he had followed her inside before she had the chance to ask him to wait outside.

Christine said nothing even well after they'd settled on her patio. She wasn't going to ask him what brought him out so early in the morning. She wasn't even going to hint at her plans, by asking the town's only realtor why he'd bother hurrying out to her place just a few days after she'd come to town, after so many years away.

It was obvious. She just wanted to make him work for it. To ask her first, and make clear his intentions.

"Well, I'll tell you," LaBelle finally started. "Everyone still misses your dad around here. My dad, rest his soul, considered him the best Lucid had to offer. He would have said that at your dad's funeral had he been asked to speak."

No resentment there, Christine thought sarcastically. As the bereaved daughter, she was offended that LaBelle would make such a slight known. She didn't betray her feelings, still keeping her thoughts to herself. Still, she wanted him to get to his point. He was wasting her precious time, apparently thinking he had all the time in the world.

"You sure surprised everyone in town by coming up here. I see you've got the house all shaped up already."

He'd already been assessing the place's sales potential, how much work it might take to get the maximum profit. But how would he know what she'd done to it, she thought, to shape it up? Of course, she instantly realized. He likely had the same access to the property as everyone else. He had also likely been keeping tabs on its potential for a profitable, and quick, sale for quite a while, biding his time until she finally showed up.

"Your dad was pretty savvy. He put together a fine spread here. I hope you don't mind I've come up here from time to time—"

Why, yes, I do mind, but she kept that again to herself.

"—just to take in the view of course. My dad brought me out here when I was a kid, when he'd come to visit your dad. After my dad died, it was nice to come out here and remember the two of them together."

"Right," she said, tempering her unplanned sarcasm with a softer remark. "I'm sure that gave you some comfort." He seemed not to notice her initially sarcastic tone. Not that he let on if he did.

He smiled. "You make a fine cup of coffee." His eyes lingered a fraction too long on her again, and not just on her eyes. He'd taken in every bit of her appearance, evaluating what her body might be worth, in addition to all of the surrounding property.

"I hear you're planning on staying here for a few weeks?"

"Could be a few weeks," she said without a trace of coldness in her voice. She'd at least managed a neutral tone, even though she was growing more repulsed by the minute. "Maybe a few weeks after that. I haven't really decided yet."

"This is quite a lot of property to take care of," he said, "Though judging by the sight of you up on that ladder," he gave her legs the once-over, again, "I'm sure that a single lady is used to taking care of a lot of things by herself."

The way he phrased the last sentence made it sound as suggestive as possible. He licked his lips once again.

"How's your wife by the way?" Christine said, making the point of inventorying his obvious wedding ring. "Meridee, right?" Though the man made her blood go cold, she was up to the challenge of verbally slapping him, and making her lack of interest in him abundantly clear.

Ruth's younger sister had really scored by marrying a LaBelle. Meridee was the envy of every woman in town—at least her net worth was—her marriage, not so much. Christine had heard all the talk about the LaBelles over the years, and it sounded like the younger LaBelle had not changed from the leering young man she remembered from her college days in Lucid. He'd married, but that hadn't stopped him from keeping a series of girlfriends. There was no way his wife didn't know about the girlfriends. Still, she remained the wife of Lucid's most wealthy man, probably constantly weighing whether she'd do better as the ex-wife. Time would only tell.

"Yes. Meridee. She's well. She's on her annual shopping trip to Paris. Into all that fashion stuff. I've heard you made quite the fashionable entrance to the Y Not the other night. I'm sure the two of you should compare notes." He put a heavy, possessive hand on hers. "Fashion-wise," he winked. "Though I'm sure you could teach her a thing or two, her taste isn't the greatest."

Considering she chose you as a husband, Christine thought. She tugged her hand out from under his heavy one, embedding another splinter in her finger from the wooden armrest in freeing herself.

"Oh, you got a splinter. I'd be glad to help you pull it out," he offered, removing an expensive multi-attachment utility tool from its leather case on his belt. He flipped out its tweezers attachment. He didn't apologize for causing the problem in the first place.

"You should get one of these. Pretty handy for use out in this part of Minnesota. I got the heavy-duty one. Never know when I'll need to gut a fish. Or remove a pretty lady's splinter. It does both and more." He held the tweezers over her finger.

"Ah, no. I can take care of it myself." Her patience was finally at an end. "Look," she said jumping up from her chair. "I've got a lot to do around here, so let's just get to the point of your visit, which was, I'm pretty sure, not a social one."

"I'm so sorry to have interrupted your morning. Really, this was merely a social call and a chance to take in the view from here," he said. "Can you blame me?" he winked.

Yes, she did want to blame him for ruining her morning.

"And, yes, of course I did want to mention that should you be interested in selling the property, my company would help with that sale. Ruth told me that you were talking about selling the place."

The grapevine had gotten information from somewhere, somehow just tapping into her feelings?

"Actually, I didn't say anything like that to Ruth. Or anyone. I'm not sure where you're getting that information," she said, her finger throbbing. The splinter had gone in deep.

"So, you've decided not to sell then," he said, holding out the tweezers once again, then taking her hand in his. "Really that thing needs to come out before it causes even more trouble." He held on hard, squeezing her fingers together painfully in the vise-grip of his sweaty hands.

She ripped her hand away, nearly jabbing herself on the tweezers. "I said, I'll take care of it."

"Well, then," he said. "I apologize for only trying to help you. You're one stubborn lady. You haven't changed much."

Yes, she'd rebuffed his advances in the past, she recalled, his visit bringing back the uncomfortable memories she'd obviously repressed. The last one had come just one week before he married Meridee.

She wanted to state the obvious but didn't. He hadn't changed either from the greedy boy who hoped to marry, or at minimum bed, the daughter of the owner of one of Lucid's finest properties. She'd never let on to her father that LaBelle's advances included a disgusting incident where he'd groped her, openly, in front of his gang of friends. Her father may have guessed about the repulsive incident later, or heard about it through the grapevine, but that incident marked the end of her summer vacations in Lucid. Yes, she was still the same stubborn lady she'd been back in those days. Except that after that incident, he'd called her a skinny bitch, not worth his time.

That experience had resolved her career indecision. She was determined to help crime victims, those not as strong as she, to get the help they needed. By the end of the summer, she'd decided on her major, shifting from psychology to social work, determined to put herself in the service of underserved communities.

"Get to your point," she said again through gritted teeth.

"Are you?" he said, "selling? Or staying?"

"When I'm good and ready to make that intention known, I'll let you know," she said. "Until then, I'm not interested in discussing it. With anyone."

"I see," he said, his eyes calculating her again. They were the eyes of a man who'd tripled his father's estate. The eyes of a man who knew valuable property when he saw it. He was not going to give up. "If you decide to sell, please call us first," he said, handing her a business card.

She planned to call him never. He finally drove off in his brand new gigantic SUV, speeding down her driveway like it was a four-lane highway. She tore his card up and flushed it down her toilet. Her finger was still throbbing, and she found a rusty pair of tweezers in the medicine cabinet, with which she managed to extract at least part of the splinter, while further embedding the rest. The pain only hardened her resolve. The sight of the worn old ladder spurred her on. She wouldn't let this town undo her. She couldn't.

11

Mercifully, Christine and her throbbing finger were left alone for the remainder of the day. Ted had not turned up with screen repair supplies, and even though he was the closest she had to family, and the one person who seemed *might* be on her side, she had no intention of calling him to ask when he might be expected.

By dinnertime, she'd made substantial progress inventorying all of the contents of the pole barn. It hadn't taken her as long as she thought, confirming her suspicions that many items were missing. She locked the pole barn, went inside the house, and gave the kittens some quality lap time while she organized her index cards and ate the rest of Ruth's chicken.

The pain from her finger reminded her that she planned—and very much needed—to take a long relaxing bath. Giving her finger a long soak would help bring the remaining piece of splinter out, and also help to clean and disinfect the wound. She located her bottle of pricey, soothing bath oil and ran a tub of water, and while it ran, she began looking through the bathroom cupboard to see if the first aid kit was where it had been for years.

She quickly located it inside the linen cabinet above where the fresh towels were kept. She flinched when she saw the unfolded pile of clean towels. Nothing, of course, was to her folding specifications in the cupboard. She had some work to do, but later, when she was done with her bath.

She grabbed the untidy heap of towels, noticing that sheets of paper were stuck in between them. By now she'd grown used to the fact that things in her dad's place had been jumbled up. In the pole barn, for instance, plumbing tools were scattered in several places, empty fuel containers for the various mowers, boats, and snowblowers were found in all four corners, some randomly next to the machine they were intended to fuel, and not tidily stored back where they belonged.

She hadn't gotten to the bathroom linen cabinet yet. She'd merely washed and replaced the towels that had been hanging on the towel rack since the geologist left. For all she knew, the stack of papers were the missing owner's manual for the tractor, brought inside the bathroom by some unknown trespasser determined to learn how to operate the machinery while he attended to personal business on the throne.

Her father had often said he did his best thinking there.

She dumped the pile on the kitchen table, intending to organize it after she'd cleaned herself up. Or maybe she would give herself a break and get to the laborious task of folding them properly the next day. The kittens followed her to the bathroom, and Precious nearly jumped in the tub before Christine could, reminding her it was time to confine them in her dad's bedroom for the night. Even though they weren't more than six months old, they'd managed to terrorize a few mice already, not quite knowing what to do with them other than to flush them out and corner them, let them get away and start over again. At least that had helped Christine locate some spots where they appeared to be getting inside the house. She plugged the holes with steel wool, planning to more permanently address the problem later.

They'd earned her lap several times over already, even though they had already chewed the end of her favorite calf-leather belt and crawled into her suitcase to nip the spaghetti straps of a couple of camisoles. On the whole, she was fast growing comfortable with having the little troublemakers around, and thought it might be nice to have them back in Somerset Hills, when she eventually went home.

She poured a shot glass of bourbon and grabbed the Harold Robbins book from the nightstand. To hell with Chrissy's problems getting along with people in Lucid. To hell with Christine's OCD. She was going to have a good long soak and luxuriate with some quality, early 1980s trash. In moments she was swept away by the lusty novel *Goodbye, Janette*, the story of prison camp survivors Tanya and her daughters, Janette and Lauren, and their new life of high fashion and high society. Tanya, who dove into the world of haute couture, Lauren, the glamorous beauty who chose a more decadent path, and Janette, who had demons to conquer before she could be a success. Christine recalled how it was she'd been drawn to the book while going to college and deciding on her career. The 1980's had been a fervent time of possibility for young professional women who, for the first time, could have it all, though not possibly as much as Robbins's heroines.

She's just gotten to the end of the first fifty pages when a name popped into her head. Lloyd Poole. She flipped back a few pages to see if she'd missed one of the characters and that indeed there was a man named Lloyd Poole. It was an odd name to crop up at this point in the story, which at this stage had guys with German names like Schwebel and Wolfgang. There wasn't a Lloyd Poole anywhere. She kept reading and the name kept repeating itself in her mind, finally distracting her so much from what should be a completely engrossing tale, until she had to set the book down. The water had gone cold anyway. She stepped out of the tub, put on the high school jersey she was wearing as pajamas, then remembered where it was she'd spotted the name Lloyd Poole. It hadn't been in the Robbins novel, nor another of the old paperbacks sitting on the nightstand. It was in the stack of papers crammed between the towels. She hurried to the kitchen to look through the material she had thought might be a missing tractor manual.

Lloyd Poole was the name listed on the top sheet, which was a report coversheet. A company name was also listed on the coversheet. American Consolidated Oil. Lloyd Poole's title was indicated as CEO, American Consolidated Oil.

The rest of the page blurred under her eyes. It was filled with identifying codes, a listing of attachments and exhibits, study area coordinates keyed to a map attached as an addendum to the report. Christine flipped to the second page and read all the way to the bottom to see the name of the individual who wrote the report.

It was Steve Adams, chief geologist for American Consolidated Oil.

12

For the next several hours, and far into the night, Christine read and reread Adams's report, still not quite believing that indeed this was the genuine thing. The man and all of his gear, save the parka, were missing. Most of the residents of Lucid had likely been inside the house where the report had been hidden or misplaced by Adams himself before he disappeared. How could it have been possible that the report sat in the house, undiscovered, for months? Was it possible this was the only copy anywhere?

She had no way of knowing, but thought not. If someone else did have a copy, why wouldn't they have made the results known? Her concern grew that another copy or copies were out there somewhere in the world. And whoever had it was keeping the information secret.

The report itself was hard to decipher by someone with no background in shale oil. Christine could not even answer for herself, after reading and rereading the report, the most basic question. Had he found the damn oil? This was why she read it numerous times. She was trying to understand, thoroughly, what Adams was saying he had learned.

Christine wished she had a computer with her, and an Internet connection, but of course though her dad had thoroughly modernized the little house, it wasn't up to the standards of the twenty-first century—no broadband or dial-up or any other connection to the World Wide Web. She was stuck with the report in front of her, and it left her confused and uncertain. But she knew enough to realize it was providing enough specific detail to layout precisely whether there was oil, and if there was, exactly where it could be found.

She looked at the key to the map, and noted that several sample sites were on her property. No other samples were taken in other parts of Lucid. Only her dad's place had been explored by Adams. No wonder there was so much interest in her return. Everyone in town would have known that in addition to other areas of exploration, Adams had a particular interest in her property.

And since it was private property, and not government land, it would provide much better access to an oil company, much less hassle of working through a byzantine structure of government agencies to get the necessary permission. Though she wasn't familiar with oil drilling permitting, Christine worked for a government agency, and even inside it was difficult to keep up with all of the paperwork. She wondered why she hadn't been asked for her permission to allow sampling? She wondered who had given him permission? Likely Ted. That he'd never mentioned it to her really shouldn't be a shock to her. She'd taken such a hands-off approach to the affairs of Lucid and basically given him carte blanche to do what he felt necessary. He couldn't be blamed for not seeking her approval.

For all she knew, he'd sent some papers for her to initial and return. He'd sent her similar things over the years, which she signed and return without even noticing.

Did she want to be an oil baroness? If indeed that was what this report meant? That oil had been found, and significant amounts were directly on her property. She wondered if Ted knew anything. And if he had, had he passed along information to Ruth, who might have relayed it to Meridee? Once word got to Meridee, undoubtedly Greg LaBelle's interest and thirst for a piece of the action would have been piqued.

She glanced at her cell phone, thinking of calling Arvo and telling him of her find. But it was three in the morning, and she didn't really know what she had found. Had this sort of information been uncovered in her home county, she would have immediately turned it over to the authorities, not necessarily because it might be the missing link to finding Steve Adams, but because it was her obligation both as a county employee and as a citizen.

But this was Lucid. She wasn't sure what the police would do with the information. Maybe it would wind up in Greg LaBelle's lap, giving him the information he needed to potentially swindle her in a land sale. With everything that had been taken from her, the report, incomprehensible as it was to her, gave her the first real advantage. She wanted to use it to gain some kind of control over the chaos and barriers she'd encountered since first coming to town.

After rereading it again, she leaned back and realized what had happened to her. The moment she decided to keep the information to herself, hadn't she just turned into what she hated most about people she'd encountered, like Greg LaBelle? A user? Wasn't Lisa Adams more deserving of whatever the report might provide by way of locating her husband? Why had Christine's first instinct been to hoard its advantages, in particular, the advantage of being the only one with potentially explosive information?

Her head was spinning. The next time she looked at her cell phone, she saw it was 4:00 a.m. She'd gone back and forth in her head, still struggling with what to do with the report, who she could ask to help her make sense of it, who she could trust, at all, with the information. Arvo was still on vacation. Everyone she knew in Lucid had a vested interest in the results. Even Ted, as decent as he appeared to be, was far too connected—and potentially could profit—were the results made known.

Since she couldn't decide, she allowed herself more time. She located a spot inside the house that she expected would be a safe place to keep the valuable pages. By the time she at last went to bed, she closed the thick, blackout curtain she'd hung in her bedroom window, and fell into a dead sleep. While she hoped for her dreams to suggest a solution to her quandary—almost went so far as to wish for a nightmare if that's what it took—she was so exhausted by reading the undecipherable equations in Adams report that neither dream nor nightmare could take proper hold of her bewildered brain. All she dreamt of were long combinations of codes, lines upon lines of ones and zeroes parading past her in pulsating, unfathomable silence.

13

CHRISTINE ROSE UNUSUALLY LATE the next day, her room pitch black. She thought she had just fallen asleep, but glanced at her clock and saw it was nearly noon. The loud, persistent mewing of Precious and Semi-Precious alerted her to the fact that it was long past breakfast for them. She stumbled out of bed and released the two fierce mousers, who ran to their food dish, running over each other in their scramble to be fed. She got a can of cat food out of the cupboard and the ravenous felines were practically ripping it out of her hands they were so hungry.

"Sorry, guys," she said. "I guess I overslept."

Christine tossed on a pair of jeans and a t-shirt, and sat in her screen porch staring across the yard at the pole barn. She knew she was at least three cups short of being able to face another long day of inventorying but knew she needed the structure of that task to keep her focused on productive work, and not her head-spinning discovery from the night before.

There was, however, going to be another obstacle she hadn't planned on. *Jesus Christ*, she thought when she spotted the signature blue and white logo of a Lucid police department squad car. In fact, the only squad car in town. The car parked near her pole barn, and a Lucid police officer, in fact the only full-time member of the police force, Ted's replacement, slowly got out of the squad and ambled over to where Christine sat in her screen porch.

"Good afternoon, Ms. Ivory," the officer said. "I'm Officer Dent McCauley of the Lucid police department. How are you today?"

The thought of the hidden report flitted through Christine's head. If she was going to admit to having found it, she thought now was the right time. Before not admitting having it got her into deep trouble.

Maybe he already somehow knew, maybe her thoughts had been telegraphed into the grapevine, just like her unannounced plans to sell the place, and everyone in town already knew about the report.

"I'm just peachy," she said, wondering if he'd been summoned by the gossips to arrest her on the spot for concealing it from the law.

"Do you know why I might have come out here today?" Officer McCauley asked her in what he probably thought was a professional manner.

He was a young guy on the extra large side. Given the size of his enormous belly—requiring he wear two heavy-duty suspender straps to keep his pants at regulation level—the young officer was still panting after making the very short walk from his car to her screen porch. He wiped his sweating brow with a handkerchief and waited for her reply.

"Officer, why don't you tell me that?" she said, choosing not to reveal what she found. She reasoned the report had been sitting there undiscovered in her linen cabinet for six months. It wouldn't hurt for another day or two to go by without her notifying anyone that it had been found. She'd accept the consequences if the report was the reason for Officer McCauley's strenuous effort in driving the mile from town to her property, and taking the short, but difficult walk from his car to her screen porch.

"Miss Ivory, would you mind stepping outside with me so I can explain why I'm here?"

"Ah, why of course, officer. I'll only be a moment." She pointed to her feet. "Need to get some shoes on."

She stuck her bare feet into the work boots, taking time to tie them. She didn't need to have the rather large officer potentially slipping on her laces and one or both of them falling to the ground.

She glanced toward the potbelly stove where she'd hidden the report, having tucked it under a carefully arrange assortment of firewood. She could see that none of the pages were poking out.

She stepped outside and met the officer, and he walked her back to his car. He opened the door and retrieved some paper work, then pointed towards the motion detector the security company installed.

"Did you have that motion detector installed recently?" He asked. "Along with several other home security related devices, including a silent alarm?"

He held out the papers he'd retrieved from his squad car, tapping an enormous index finger on the papers to show her what they were, and whose name was prominently indicated as the owner.

She started to laugh, first quietly, then louder, then so overcome with her hysterics that she fell to her knees. She felt both relieved and exasperated. Relieved because he wasn't there to arrest her because of the hidden report. But exasperated because she knew exactly what his visit meant. Her newly installed alarm system might be entirely worthless.

"I'm sorry, officer McCauley. I know I shouldn't be laughing about this," she said, trying to recover some sense of decorum. "Yes, as those papers say, I'm clearly the person who had this deluxe security system installed. With all the bells and whistles, including the silent alarm."

"I really don't want to be let in on your little joke, no matter how funny it may be. This is serious police business I'm here to inform you about," he said.

"Yes," Christine said. "I truly and genuinely apologize for my outburst. No one feels worse about the whole damn thing than me." She tried desperately to recall if she'd finished off the Jim Beam. She was going to need a drink after Officer McCauley left.

"Ms. Ivory, when you signed off on these papers, did you notice the clause in the agreement, that you checked and initialed here," he jabbed his finger on the paper, "and again here?" he said flipping to the next page.

"Um. Yes, well those are my initials," she said. "So I did indeed agree, as my checking the 'I agree' box, and my initials signify." She knew she didn't have the foggiest notion of what she had agreed to.

"Let me refresh your memory," he said, adjusting his suspender straps and wiping off his forehead again, "in case you don't exactly recall."

He read from the new security owner agreement Christine had checked and signed in not one, but two places. "The new security owner agreement states that new security owners agree to inform their local police department, as per local ordinance, of their installation of a new home security system, including filling out new alarm user permits where required."

He went on, "I can see that you may not understand why this is so important, and why we have, in Lucid, an alarm user law. You see, the law requires an 'alarm user' (i.e. property owner, manager, or resident) to obtain an alarm-user permit, which means you must file current information with the Police Department. With this information on file, officers should be able to quickly locate a property owner, manager, resident, or alarm company representative who can join the police in responding to the alarm call," he said.

He sounded like he had the city laws memorized, and in some respects, Christine was glad to hear from a guy who was so by the book. Maybe there was hope that he could help her find and bring to justice people who had taken her things. Count on him when she needed him. Arvo was, after all, far away and on vacation. And out of her life.

"Now," he said, "This is a somewhat new law. It's only been on the books for five years. But I'm here to inform you that when the law went into effect, it applied to everyone, even people who had alarm systems for many years. To be honest," he said, "not many people install such elaborate systems up here. They tend to look out for each other. It's a pretty close-knit community."

Yeah, she thought. *Determined to keep things the way they are, meaning that no one new is permitted inside that community.*

"Since you've obviously only recently installed the devices, and are possibly not aware of the consequences, I thought it best to come out here and inform you myself. The ordinance has fees for permit renewal, fees to cover responses to false alarms, and a fine for a false alarm from an unpermitted alarm system," he pointed out. "See that's where the law directly applies to you today."

"I see," Christine said, feeling duly informed of the potential for a fine.

"Further," he went on, wiping his forehead again, "While there is no fee for police response to alarms triggered by criminal activity, alarm users are charged a fee for the second and subsequent false alarms," he said. "See that last part is the part that applies to me, too."

"Because you're the guy, if I'm understanding this right," she said, "who gets the call in the middle of the night when the alarm goes off. Night or day, the call comes into you."

"Miss Ivory, I'm glad you understand exactly why the ordinance was passed into law in the first place. Yes, you are exactly right. I'm the first responder to these things."

"Probably sometimes the only responder?" she asked.

"Pretty much all the time the only responder to these things."

"Ah. I'm getting the whole picture," she said. Truly, her alarm system was completely useless. She had learned she most likely could not trust anyone inside Lucid, not the old cop, and not the new one. Should her alarm go off, would she indeed be able to rely on the local cops to respond to it? Or would they only consider it a nuisance, just like her, and ignore it. Maybe this was why Ted hadn't said a thing to her when he'd been out the previous day. He knew exactly what would happen if the thing went off.

"Well, let me make sure you understand. See, like you, I'm relatively new in town."

Ah ha, she thought. Maybe he hasn't gone over to the dark side yet.

"I take my job very seriously. But I'm just one guy. I answer all the calls. I'm getting to know the people, and the town, and I'm not even close to having my finger on the pulse of what makes things tick around here. So for right now I have to follow up on every request that comes in, all of the alarms, even the false ones, keep the peace in a community where I'm the newest member, making sure everyone is safe. I really don't have time for false alarms see—this is a lot of responsibility for one person, and I need to make every second count," he said, hiking up his pants again, and setting the paperwork on the hood of his car.

"And when an alarm goes off, and I don't have any information about the owner, well what am I supposed to do? I still need to locate the owner, figure out if there is a problem. It goes off, and based on my experience with home alarm systems—especially out here in the countryside—nine times out of ten it's a false alarm. Maybe a deer has tripped the alarm. The owner accidentally sets it off. Or the owner's kid, crawling in his window way past when he should have."

He startled her with an unexpected analogy. "An alarm is like the town gossip, you know? Most of the time you can ignore it, it's a bunch of noise that people use to make themselves look better, others look worse, establish their position in the community. Problem is that one in ten times there's a hidden truth that needs to be teased out and followed up on. Well, you just can't ignore it. I mean *I* can't ignore it. And believe me, I won't," he said. "Like some of that terrible bullying that goes on nowadays. It's normal for kids to pick on other kids, that's what someone will tell me, kind of making it seems like it's no problem to call another person names, just because they're different. Well, some people can take it, dish it back, not be affected by it. But the ones who can't . . . well, those are the people I never want to ignore. Especially the ones who don't ask for help."

"Officer," Christine said, stopping him. "I really do understand exactly what you're telling me." She knew where he was coming from. The guy seemed genuine. "I really thank you for coming out here to explain all of this to me. I'm sorry I didn't follow the ordinance."

She quickly gave him the rest of the information he needed. Her cell phone number, home address, past and future employer information. He of course duly informed her that that complete information was needed in case the alarm went off and she was not in town.

"Before you leave, may I ask you a question?" Christine said.

"Of course, ma'am."

"When did you start with the Lucid police department?" She asked even though she already knew the answer.

"This past spring, ma'am. When Officer Nelson retired. Officer Nelson was on the job for a very long time and, as I understand it, reluctantly retired last spring. I was proud and pleased to be hired fresh out of school. Officer Nelson was a very fine officer, so I have big shoes to fill."

"So, you're really new to all of this: Lucid and your job?"

"Yes, ma'am, I am, but I can assure you I'm very well qualified for the job." He gave her a thorough run down on his education and job history, and she listened politely to where he obtained his degree and his various certifications.

"May I ask you just one more thing?" she said.

"Certainly, ma'am."

"I don't recognize your last name as a Lucid family name. Are you originally from Lucid?" she asked.

"No, ma'am. I'm not. I was born and raised in the southeastern part of the state. La Crescent?"

"Yes. I'm familiar with La Crescent. It's way down in the southeast corner. Kind of more in my neck of the woods. Just downriver from Somerset Hills."

"Yes, ma'am. That's right. I went to Pelican Falls Technical College for law enforcement training. I don't know anyone around here, but I'm working hard to get to know them. I came from a small town, so I know it takes some time for new people to be accepted. But really, they're like people everywhere. Some bad apples, but for the most part decent people. Law-abiding citizens."

"Well, you've obviously studied up on the city laws here."

"It's my job, ma'am."

"Of course. Yes, it's your job," she was beaming by then. "And with that, I won't keep you any longer from your job. Thank you, again, for coming out. It was a genuine pleasure to get to know you."

"Thank you, ma'am," he said, squeezing his XXXXL frame back into the squad car. He turned on the engine and said out the window, "I hope the rest of your day is a good one."

Son of a biscuit, Christine thought, using a mild expletive she'd often heard her dad use. But that was what happened to her when she spent time in his hometown.

"Son of a biscuit," she said as loudly as she could, startling all the goldfinches off the bird feeder. After the terrible night she'd had, things couldn't have seemed bleaker. But now she was feeling more positive than she had the entire time she'd been in Lucid. She hoped, and believed, that she had found one person she might be able to trust in town. And she was thanking her lucky stars that it was possible that Lucid's current police force, in the very large figure of officer Dent McCauley, might come down on her side, if she needed him. Maybe she was going to survive the ordeal after all, if only for the next week or so.

14

Ted arrived late that afternoon, with a truckload of items he'd rounded up. He met her as she was just coming out of the pole barn, clipboard in hand. His look matched hers, neither looked happy with the other.

Christine spotted something poking out of the tangle of items, and her eyes lit up. "The tractor wrench!" Christine said, clapping her hands with glee when he pulled an oversized wrench out of his truck bed.

"You know what that is?" he asked.

"Well, of course!" she said. "You need it if you have a tractor. The lawn needs mowing, and I thought I'd get the tractor out this afternoon and give it a trim."

"Oh," he said. "That's right. I remember your dad teaching you how to drive it," he said. "Of course, back then you weren't quite tall enough to reach everything." His eyes fell onto the clipboard, and saw her detailed, handwritten inventory.

"What?" she asked, noting his souring look.

"What's that?" he said, pointing at her list.

She wasn't sure she could evade his questions, so she decided to meet him head on. "I was . . ."

"You were trying to see if you had all of your precious, unused stuff," he said, "right? What were you going to do, come after us with an expensive city lawyer, maybe have us all hauled off to court?"

She spat out, "Of course not," without thinking. She had enough respect for her dad at least to try not to have his best friend completely furious with her. But it looked too late. She backtracked, trying to throw a cold bucket of water of the first flames of a bridge burning. "I just need to find out what's what. If I decide to sell, I'd probably have all the stuff out there auctioned off. I need to know what I have."

"I remember your ridiculous system of index cards—making your dad come after us with those stupid things. Most of us just laughed when he would hand them around. You know what he did?" Ted asked her, his voice shaking.

"What?" she asked, not having ever considered how those transactions went.

"He said that you were only trying to be helpful," Ted said. "That you didn't understand how things worked."

He went on. "Of course, we wondered why he didn't try and help you to understand. He would just shrug his shoulders and say there was no point in trying to get you to change your mind, once it was made up."

She smiled, a little ruefully.

"Even if the idea was so ridiculous. Well, though none of us liked it, a few things might get handed over, but on principle we just waited until you left town, then maybe returned his stuff. Honestly you could be so stubborn. Such a pain. Just like your dad. That man was determined to get the price he wanted, whether that was on more acreage or equipment, or the big fish he was after, but he was far more subtle than you. More patient, that was for sure. The guy knew how to wait. You could help yourself by trying to be patient."

She didn't want to point out she'd already tried something else he'd suggested. The sugar approach. She found it hadn't worked.

"And I suppose I can't talk you out of mowing the lawn by yourself. One or the other of us has kept up with that, for years, without your help."

"Like I said. It's time for me to step up and handle things," she said. "I intend to do that."

"Well," he said, "suit yourself. I do intend to fix your screen today, just like I told you I would. And I won't be talked out of it," he said. "So don't even start." He gave her a hard look.

That was all he said to her, and he set to returning all the things to their rightful place in the pole barn. She had seen that most of the items she'd already discovered were missing—the ladders, wrenches, and chainsaws, were all there. She could see that he wasn't planning on saying another word to her until he was finished.

Clearly he was angry with her. He'd given her a piece of his mind with no interruption from her, and she knew better than to offer up another apology. She didn't want to, anyway. She was in the right, Lucid was wrong. Carting off half her dad's belongings with no apparent obligation to attempt to get her permission, or return the items when they were finished.

She made a mental note to check the pole barn later, after Ted had finally gone. She went inside the house, determined to finish her inventory there. She was finished placating, supplicating herself to the town's collective judgment of her: guilty until proven innocent. They had it all wrong.

She wasn't entirely sure she agreed with officer McCauley. Almost all of her experiences had showed her the bad side of people. She stomped around her kitchen, furious with everyone, sent her clipboard slamming against the countertop. A kitten squealed when her heavy boot landed on a tail. Precious, the tabby, ran off and hid under the potbelly stove, looking at her with fearful eyes.

"Damn it, Precious," she said, not sure whether she was more upset that the cat had startled her in crying out than she was for hurting the little thing. "Oh, for chrissakes, come on out. I'm sorry I hurt you."

Christine sat still, and when Semi Precious showed up to take advantage of her available lap, Precious joined quickly after, and in no time, both kittens were purring in a heap on her lap. "You two have that sugar thing down, don't you?" Maybe she could learn something from them, she thought, as she stroked their little heads and scratched the little chins that pressed eagerly for just that.

She sighed, knowing she had a duty to stay right there with the pair of them on her lap. While they helped calm her down, they didn't give her the one thing she really needed. That comfortable sense of where the equivalent place was for her, the security of knowing and trusting she were where she'd be taken care of. Her dad's place used to offer that kind of sanctuary to her, misguided as her attempts to structure were. Her dad never let on the reception he'd gotten when he'd gone and confronted people, on her insistence, to reclaim his property. Ted made it clear. No one had wanted her interference in the town's informal barter structure, where people helped themselves to what they needed, with the understanding that the other would get what he or she needed when the time came.

It was an unstructured, flexible system of give and take. She wasn't capable of operating under those conditions. The loose accounting didn't make sure that the system was fair or balanced. Based on what she'd experienced, more had been taken from her, and not much given back.

She remembered Arvo telling her to keep an open mind. And with that, it came to her. That she actually had been on the receiving end. Ted, and possibly others, had been giving, and quite a bit actually.

She heard the sound of the tractor starting up without any sputters. Instead of jumping to the conclusion that Ted was doing exactly what she'd asked him not to do, the opposite occurred to her. The tractor was working perfectly, but precisely because he, or someone else in town, had been taking care of it these past ten years.

She had been so busy looking for things that weren't there, noticing only what was missing, that she had completely missed the truth all around her, of what had been done, and done right. She gently set the kittens on her father's bed and walked outside, her heart more open than it had been just moments ago, probably for the first time since she'd arrived. She stepped back to the edge of the lawn and watched the elderly retired cop doing what he'd likely done many times over the past decade. He was carefully driving up and down the edge of the driveway, mowing the lawn.

She noticed something else she'd missed, as she looked at the house. The roof had been recently replaced. The gutters and flashing were all new. She hadn't even noticed until that moment, but remembered her father mentioning, shortly before he died, that it was something he'd meant to get to. He hadn't. But someone else had, most likely the old man out there riding on the aging, but well cared for tractor.

She realized why it was so easy for her to key in on what was gone. She touched the side of her face, not having noticed until she pulled her finger back and looked at the wet tip, that she was crying. The significant absence from her life these past ten years: the loss of her father, her unfinished grieving, was what had her focused only on the negatives, the negative space, that emptiness in her heart that had not been adequately recovered since the end of his life.

The old man drove the tractor back into the pole barn and carefully parked it. She watched him carrying a roll of screen and other tools to the screen porch, kneeling down, with difficulty, to tackle the next task.

The real problem went beyond who was absent from Christine's life. She'd been deficient all her life, really, never knowing how to let others take care of her and be thankful when they did. The word struck her. Thanks. She realized that she had not once mentioned her appreciation to Ted, for everything he'd done in taking care of the place. In taking care of her really. She'd not once said thanks to him.

Until that moment, she'd been completely blinded to the hardness that she knew existed inside her, but clearly had never seen the full impact of it. Yet, there he was, not thanked even once, still taking care of things for her. Maybe out of respect for her dad, but, it was just possible, for her, a woman who'd come home to a place where she had roots, to the place where her father was buried.

She watched the old man taking the torn screen off, measuring the replacement, and securely putting the new screen back in place. She needed all the time it took for him to complete his work to think through how, on earth, she was going to apologize this time, make it seem as genuine and as heartfelt as it needed to be, and somehow begin to earn his respect, once more.

She knew the answer might be hidden deep inside of her, and wondered if she had the time to make that answer emerge and make sense. She thought she'd start with what she knew, even though it was so difficult for her to take a chance, move ahead without being intellectually ready, but knowing only in her heart the right thing to do. She saw he was finishing up, and asked him to please come inside her house, she had difficult words she needed to share with him. She could no longer wait for Arvo to provide her with evidence that would allow her to trust the man. Her father had. That was good enough.

She poured the two final shot glasses of Jim Beam, and first said, through tears, for the very first time, how deeply she wanted to thank the man and how foolish she'd been. When she was certain he understood the depth of her sincerity, she told him there was something else she'd been keeping from him.

She walked to the potbelly stove, removed the carefully arranged pile of wood, and handed him what she'd hidden inside the potbelly stove. As much as she'd been thrown off balance by Lucid's way of doing things, and as much as she dreaded the thought of how Lucid was going to be thrown off by the report's implications of the hidden report, she revealed its existence to one of two people in the world she had learned, only through heartbreak, that she could trust.

15

Ted read through the report, just as Christine had done the day before. When he'd gotten to the end, he glanced at her incredulous, started to say something to her about it, then shook his head and began again, from the beginning. Christine knew then that he was having the same experience she had.

The sense of overwhelmed disbelief. How reading the report gave one a sense of connection to Adams, his methodical thought process.

She expected he'd have the same need to read through it several times. She hoped it would make more sense to him than it had to her. Maybe in the time spent chatting with Adams before the man disappeared, Ted had gained enough knowledge to understand the basic process Adams had gone through in conducting his study of the area.

She caught a glimpse of a tear in Ted's eye. The men had grown closer than she suspected. He might have been experiencing the kind of response she had when she first set foot on her dad's property after being away so long. She could feel her father's presence everywhere, and had to, in a way, go through grief anew every time she opened another cabinet and touched objects that were last touched by him, a decade earlier. For every object she found, there was a story. A chipped mug that really couldn't be used any longer, unless you wanted to cut your lip every time you took a sip, but also couldn't be discarded because it was his favorite. And the reason it was his favorite was that it had been a gift from Christine some Christmas years ago. Her expired fishing licenses, one for each summer she spent with him, had been preserved. Her tackle box, just as neatly organized as would be expected, with the sure-fire Rapala lures, color coordinated by Christine.

Though Adams wasn't family to Ted, it was clear the man had grown on him. Holding the report in his hands was the first contact he'd had in months.

"It's like he's sitting right here with me," Ted said. "I told you we used to have a drink or two out on the patio," he mused. "I can hear the guy's voice, like he's reading this to me, telling me what he found."

When he got through the second time, he looked up.

"Well," she said. "I couldn't make head or tails of it Does it make any sense to you?"

"I think so," he said. "But I really need to look at it a couple more times. Does anyone else know about this report?"

"No one else," she said. She'd hoped to talk to Arvo about it, but there hadn't been time, and she knew he was still on vacation. "Just you, me, and whoever stuck the report where I found it."

"That would most likely have been Adams," he said. He got up from Christine's kitchen table and stepped outside.

"Yeah," she heard him say on the phone, "Still out at Chrissy's. It's going to be awhile . . . I know, Ruthie," he said. "I should have called sooner . . . What's that? Yeah, I know. I guess I'm still on cop time, but I've been getting better showing up for dinner for a couple of weeks now haven't I? I'm sure Joey will take care of my portion of the roast. Chrissy is already making dinner for me," he said, glancing inside the kitchen window and winking at Christine, who hadn't so much as looked inside of her refrigerator.

The look of confusion on her face evaporated—the challenge of coming up with sustenance for Ted set her on the course she'd need to keep occupied. Frankly she was so relieved that she had revealed the secret inside her house that she was prepared to celebrate, even if it meant running into town to get a few things. She would do her best, though, to scrounge up a meal, and avoid running into someone who'd blab to someone else who'd eventually tell Ruth about it.

"Yeah, she said she owes me, big time, and I couldn't turn her down."

He finally hung up and came inside. "Ruthie hates boxing up leftovers, but you'd think she'd be used to it now. Twenty years of living with the town's only cop meant a lot of last minute changes, a lot of cold dinners I'd reheat, late."

"So, I guess I'll get that dinner started I owe you," Christine said, assuring him she was glad he was staying. Ted said it was enough to have created havoc for one woman's meal plan, so he was pleased that Christine could accommodate him.

"You're right," she said. "I do owe you more than one meal." He'd mowed her lawn and fixed her screen. She knew there were countless other tasks he'd probably taken on over the years.

Ted settled in to another read-through while she went about the business of making dinner. She had just the basics in her fridge, but guessed she had plenty of time, given how absorbed Ted was working his way through the report.

She wondered if he'd come to the same conclusion she did. Though the pages were dense with tables of statistics and figures, and numerous footnotes and attachments, she'd been startled by the summary on the final page or so. The summary was so unexpected and direct, and given her solid footing in science, and her over-prepared, over-analytical, and over-organized way of doing things, she had all the basic elements to understand a scientific analysis like Adams's report. Still, she couldn't understand how Adams had arrived at his conclusion. A little more geological knowledge might have helped her align his conclusion with the meat of the report.

Things just seemed off to her somehow. Like the result didn't sync up with the facts he'd presented. She'd seen this kind of contradiction in her work. Facts not supporting someone's conclusion. Often times it just meant that the evidence wasn't solid enough to justify bringing someone to court, even if everyone *knew* otherwise. Usually what everyone *knew* was wrong. And the facts were correctly supporting the truth, it was just the opposite of what everyone had hoped.

This was particularly thorny in closed cases. She remembered Arvo telling her about a disappearance, and eventual murder, of a boy, taken at gunpoint in front of two other young witnesses, boys that wound up in her office. Arvo'd interviewed them when their memories were sharp and detailed, and everything seemed to point to a person-of-interest in the next town. The man wound up killing himself after being tormented by neighbors who were sure he was responsible, given how the boy's description matched his appearance.

Arvo had never thought that the guy was responsible, even though everyone wanted to see the boy's killer come to justice. Sure enough, the real murderer was located in a Montana jail cell, where he was serving time for a similar, later crime.

Conclusions had to be supported by facts.

Was the shale-oil conclusion everyone expected and hoped for supported by the facts that Adams laid out? That was what she hoped she'd be able to understand by reading the report. What she hoped Ted would understand. If only Adams was there to make sense of it all.

She had, however, a more pressing worry. What to feed the hungry man whose stomach was audibly growling, though he seemed unaware of it as he was so caught up in the report. She got going on her contribution to his effort, remembering that her father had always kept a garden behind the pole barn on a sunny patch of ground. She inventoried her refrigerator and pantry, and started preheating the oven while she stepped outside to investigate.

She hadn't gardened in years. Everything she knew about gardening she'd learned watching her dad fuss over the only piece of his land he actually farmed himself. Though nothing would have been planted in years, she hoped that a few perennials had come back, though it was likely the entire plot had been taken over by weeds.

She wasn't prepared for the unexpected bounty. Someone had continued to plant and tend the garden. Yet another example of what was right there in front of her, cared for and tended, but that she'd missed when she'd been on such a mission to find what was wrong, what had been taken from her. Blinded by rage, she went looking for evidence of wrong-doing, suspecting everyone of having taken advantage of her absence. The thoughtfully tended garden, freshly planted with carrots, small tomato plants, several varieties of vining beans and protected from browsing deer and rabbits by a wire fence told her how wrong she had been. The evidence that it had been cared for over the course of ten years showed in the asparagus patch she'd remembered helping plant years before and the thick hedgerow of slow-growing boxwood she remembered only coming to her knees when she helped plant them in her late teens. The boxwood hedge was now chest high, and pruned into a thick, solid rectangular windbreak.

She wondered whether it was Ruthie, known for her green thumb, who'd done most of the work? Maybe the retired cop was taking more of a role managing now, not used to having time on his hands given his retirement the past spring. She remembered there'd always been more the garden produced than that a single retired guy could use, even when his daughter was staying with him. They'd routinely brought in contributions to the town's food shelf. Christine remembered having suggested they set up a roadside stand, and maybe make a little extra money selling vegetables they didn't need.

Her dad had scolded her. Anyone who could afford to buy from them, more than likely had the same produce from their own gardens. Those in need and probably unable to pay were the ones needing their garden's excess.

She reddened thinking of how selfish she'd been then. Ruefully she reflected she hadn't changed.

She returned with an armload of freshly harvested crops: shoots of asparagus, scallions, spinach, snow peas, parsley, oregano and basil. She made a second trip, bringing a bowl and a hand trowel she fetched from the pole-barn. She pulled up an armload of rhubarb. She knew there would be plenty of time to prepare what the garden had given her.

The next time Ted looked up, it was because he smelled the delicious aroma coming from the oven. "Oh, my god," he said, his eyes wide. "Rhubarb crisp?"

She nodded.

"Something else I can't name, but I don't care what it is, I'm eating all of it."

"Well then come and get it, I was just ready to take it out of the oven. Dinner's ready for you if you're ready for it."

"Yes. I'd like some time to digest what I think I read here," he said, gathering the report pages back together and setting them aside.

She knew when he had considered everything that needed to be considered, he would tell her. There was no point in rushing him. He could be as stubborn as Christine, but in his own way. Christine knew that his years as a cop would have taught him that all the evidence needed to be collected. He wasn't the one deciding whether a person was guilty or innocent, he was there to facilitate the judgment, not rush it.

Neither of them said a word while they ate the simple dinner Christine had prepared: a baked egg dish filled with fresh asparagus and spinach and flavored with the herbs she'd collected. Steamed peapods flavored with a hint of thyme. When Ted cleaned his plate, she took it away and dished up the bubbling rhubarb crisp, its tangy sweetness the perfect accompaniment to the egg dish.

"I'm not usually a white-wine guy, but this is great," he said, holding up his glass for her to refill with the Riesling she'd found the next town over.

"I do remember that your dad never ate so well as he did when you were in town," he said. "Even as a kid, you were the best cook around."

He pushed his chair away from the table, sighed, then his expression darkened. He glanced at the report, and Christine knew it was time. Ted got up, led the way to the patio, and she followed with the wine bottle in hand. It was a beautiful evening in Lucid. High puffy clouds betraying no thought of rain. A cool breeze rising from the valleys. If there was shale oil beneath her feet, the land was giving no clue, at least to those without a geological background.

"Well, that had to be the most confusing thing I ever looked at. And believe me, I've seen a lot of confusing long documents. Most of them reports I had to file for arrests I'd made, tickets I'd given. Sometimes the strangest thing would happen. It felt like I had to be even more thorough to clear someone, you know?"

"I'm not quite sure I'm following you," Christine said.

"See, this is why Adams and I hit it off right away. Without explaining exactly where he was headed in his study, he told me that he saw this was a situation where he needed to be extra thorough. And by looking at his report, I can tell he did just that. I know the kind of situation he's talking about. A case where you might have to make an unpopular call. In a town like this, where everyone is in everyone else's business, and there are a few powerful people calling all the shots, I've run into what I think it was that made the guy certain he really needed to do his homework. You know, show his work, like they have kids do on math tests. Solve it from every possible angle."

"What did you mean by that part about 'clearing' someone?" She had a hunch that despite all the confusing detail in the report, he'd understood what she had from it, but kept dismissing because it seemed the opposite of what all the detail might have been supporting.

"Well, you know how often people who are really guilty plead innocent? As much as the accused has to defend themselves against the accumulation of evidence, sometimes what I found was that clearing a truly innocent person, whom everyone had turned against—for whatever reason—seemed to require twice the work. I always thought it was me until I came across this report. Maybe I was protecting myself by going overboard—knowing that if someone got off that everyone would have preferred be hung—well, maybe people were going to come after me, accuse me of not having done my job."

He scratched his chin and took another sip of wine. For once, Christine didn't feel pressured to hurry him on, to get to his conclusion. So she just let him talk, and helped herself to another glass. He'd figured it out, she knew. Now he needed to bring the light he'd found up to the surface, just like Adams had done in taking deep, long buried samples of the earth, slowly savoring his evaluation of the various samples, unwilling to let go of the thought process, the years of experience, the layered accumulation of knowledge, intuition, years in the field. Both men probably had approached retirement in the same way: not weary at all of their work, retirement seemed more like the death of their most engaging relationship.

"I don't know, it might have something to do with the approach I had to adopt in town. You know, lots of community relations. Good community relations, I hoped, would pave the way for people to live together. But sometimes there are people out there who aren't visible, and somehow that makes them less deserving of getting a fair shake. You know who I'm talking about?"

"Oh, I know," Christine said. "Most of my clientele are those kinds of people. The type most ordinary folk wish they could just forget about. They require lots of resources at the county level and average middle-class people don't always like that. I could 'educate' everyone until I'm blue in the face, but if I spend my time doing that, I'm spending less time doing the job of helping them out of the rut they're in." She knew exactly what he was talking about, but not where he was headed.

"See, that's what I'm talking about. More effort is required, more money, and the people with means forget that nine times out of ten, the money is going towards helping completely innocent people, most of the them kids, you know, born into a lifestyle they didn't chose. And I'm left to educate them why I didn't maybe come over and help them solve a dispute with their neighbor, who'd let his lilacs creep under the fence into their yard. How am I supposed to even begin to explain how insensitive they are being, when I've just hurried from getting a couple of kids to social services because the mom and dad were too busy making—and taking—meth in the kitchen to notice that baby's diaper hadn't been changed in a couple of days, the toddler was eating dog food, and the dog had crapped all over the house because they'd stopped taking it out." He stopped, almost too exasperated to continue. "It bugged the hell out of me that I was asked to defend the defenseless, but I did. Still it was hard for people to listen to talk about the poor underclass. They didn't want to hear it."

"You had to take the time and effort, more than usual, because people had already made a judgment and they were too close-minded to accept anything else."

"Right," he said. "Now I know it's a bit of a stretch to switch from kids born to meth-addicts to shale oil exploration, but I'm going to try and get there. People make up their minds about someone's guilt without so much as a shred of evidence, and it takes a lot of doing to convince them otherwise. That there's nothing there. Let me ask you, just gut instinct after reading the report," he said.

"I was really confused," Christine said. "Honestly, I'm just not sure. I could barely understand most of it."

"You're a smart girl, Chrissy," he said, his eyes narrowed. "I know you had some kind of opinion after reading it. Just spit it out. Did Adams find oil or not?"

She took a deep breath and said at last what she thought, even though she wasn't close to sure she understood how all the evidence added up.

"No," she said. "Based on the summary and the little bit I understood, I think there's nothing down there."

"Well, I can tell you I did spend some time with the guy, asking him about how he went about his study, so maybe the terminology is a bit more familiar to me."

"And? What did you think?" she said.

"The reason the report was so long, the research was so time-consuming, was that he knew people hoped and believed the opposite was true. He needed to have everything pretty well buttoned up, so that once he was done out here, he was done. The evidence looked pretty conclusive in there."

"No oil?" she asked again.

"Not a drop," he said. "Not one blessed drop."

16

"TELL ME WHAT HAPPENED WHEN the guy disappeared," Christine said. It was nearing ten. The twilit sky brushed india-ink washes behind backlit clouds, the sun hidden below the horizon, but still making its influence known. The solstice had arrived, its presence witnessed the veiling of night in gathering clouds.

"How'd anyone know the guy was even missing?" she asked. "You knew he was leaving. You were the last one to see him. How'd you hear that he hadn't turned up?"

"I got the call from the Charleston PD. Lisa called to report he hadn't showed up in Charleston. She'd been expecting him to fly in. She said he hadn't called to say there'd been a delay, or his flight had been cancelled, or anything like that. But she said he usually didn't keep that close in touch. It was his office that let her know if any significant delay was expected. She hadn't heard anything so as far as she knew, he'd gotten on his plane on time."

"Sounds like a long-married couple. Both living pretty independently. Not terribly involved in each other's business, except when they wanted to be."

"Yeah. They were both planning to retire this year. She worked in the school system, a principal, I think. It was her last year. His too, though I remember him telling me he wasn't all too sure about how things were going to work with both of them retired." Ted laughed.

"What's so funny?"

"I just remembered. He had outfitted a retirement place in a resort town in the mountains. What was it now? The Snowshoe Mountains. That was it. But she had no plans to sell their house in Charleston and move there full time. He was planning on just that, having a wife who visited him on the weekends."

"Sounds like they would pretty much continue with the same lifestyle they had when the both of them were working. I'm guessing he traveled quite a bit."

"Yes, he did. He asked me how I thought things would go when I retired—with Ruth. He was wondering how I'd managed to avoid the inevitable. Getting married, he meant. He said he loved his wife, liked being married, but wasn't sure that the two were always compatible. Being married and loving someone he meant."

"It sounds like the two of you got to know each other pretty well."

"I guess so, for a couple of old guys. We bonded over the retirement discussion, I'd have to say. He was looking forward to it, and it sounded like he had things pretty well figured out." He mused about these thoughts, saying nothing for several minutes.

Christine wondered if he lost his train of thought. She glanced to see his profile in the dim light, his face full of thoughts about life after retirement, perhaps whether it had met his expectations so far. She was sorry to have to move him beyond what appeared to be a peaceful place for him.

"So what happened next, after word got back here that he hadn't turned up in Charleston?" She felt the need to prompt him to continue.

She saw his eyes again focus on the previous winter.

"I came out here of course, pretty much right after the call came in, but by then a few days had already gone by. We'd had quite a bit of snow, and the driveway was pretty well impassable. In fact, right after Adams was supposed to have left, we were under a blizzard warning, and I wondered whether he was going to get out. His plan was to fly a commuter plane out of Fargo to Chicago, and hop on a flight to Charleston from there. We had talked about the weather, now that I think of it. How it was looking bad. He wondered if his flight out of Fargo was going to be cancelled. He didn't seem terribly concerned. He'd been through a lot of flight delays given the amount of travel he did. He was eager to get home, but wondering enough about that next phase of his life that a short delay probably wouldn't have bothered him too much."

"Do you know if flights were cancelled?" She was trying to remember the period he was talking about—just before the previous Christmas. But snowstorms in western Minnesota, even the bad ones, could be so frequent that it often seemed to people from Minneapolis that the winter for this remote part of the state consisted of one, long, unending blizzard warning.

"They did shut down the Fargo airport as I recall, for most of the day, but I didn't really know what flight he was supposed to have been on. The guy was a frequent flyer. Who knows, he might have been able to swing a deal getting out of there early. But after the fact, we learned he never made it to the Fargo airport: the flight log didn't list him as having checked in."

"So, I got my snowmobile out when I heard he was missing, and came out here. I had to wait until the white-out conditions ended, matter of fact. I was hoping and praying no one was going to call in having gone into labor, or had a heart attack. Those are the kind of storms where they shut down the interstate between here and the North Dakota border. Nothing gets through. The roads weren't yet cleared around here so the only tracks that showed between here and town were the ones made by snowmobiles.

"Snow was waist deep at the house windows. I could see that the truck the guy rented was gone. I looked through the windows and saw that all of his things were gone. At that time I didn't notice the Jim Beam or the coat. It just looked like there was no sign of him at the house. Given that the vehicle wasn't there, I called

West Virginia and told them he wasn't in Lucid. As I said, things were still pretty much shut down between here and Fargo, and the police and county authorities were alerted between here and there, given the guy's and the truck's description, but nothing turned up. That was the end of it for me. Until you showed up in town, and we went in there, I had no idea the guy's coat was left behind. And he'd never touched that bottle of Jim Beam."

She asked whether he knew if any investigation was ongoing. "Not as far as I know," he said, "but Carlson County took the lead."

Christine wanted to ask more. "Doesn't it seem suspicious?"

"What?" Ted said.

"That there's just nothing—everything had disappeared—when so many people were clamoring, weren't they? To know exactly what he'd found out here?" she said, pointing at the report. "The guy doesn't turn up, yet it doesn't exactly seem like this is a time when everything can be put on hold? You know, when another oil baron is being minted every day in North Dakota?"

"I wish I knew more than what I know," Ted said.

"Well Lisa Adams is certainly done waiting for answers. She seems to think more can be found out here."

"You know who else was on me every day about the missing guy? Greg LaBelle." Ted considered the information he passed along. "The guy can be pushy, no question. But he'd get downright irritated with me if I didn't tell him everything I knew."

"He was out here the other day, too. Ready to 'help me' sell my land." And help her remove it like it was a painful splinter in her thumb. "Did you tell him anything?"

"What could I say? I knew nothing. Carlson County was taking the lead, and a few months later I retired. Not that the pressure ended from Greg. He just moved onto another topic. Asking me about your land. He even set Ruth on me and then she was pestering me to talk to you about it."

Ted admitted. "For months. She even went so far as to tell me I should buy it myself. What does she think I am? Made of money? She's a good woman, but only as long as she avoids her sister. Which is not going to be happening anytime soon."

"Well, LaBelle seems to have plenty of land," Christine said. "Not sure why he needs mine. Of course it will be the last thing I'll do, selling to that creep. Why do you suppose he was so interested in the investigation?" Christine had her growing suspicions about LaBelle, but was keeping them to herself. She wanted to hear from Arvo.

"There's been talk that he's had some money problems, since the housing bust," Ted said. "More than talk actually. Did you notice that half-finished industrial park on the way into town?"

She had noticed the elaborate sign announcing the Lucid Industrial Corridor. "I didn't see much more than a sign and a big hole."

"That was it. The guy invested millions trying to attract even more millions. Sold everyone on the idea that oil was coming. Now he's got a lot of big holes where his big dreams have buried themselves. Still, he talks a big game. Not that he knows what we know. His other scheme is probably what brought him out here. He seemed most interested in acquiring the land he'd seen Adams testing. Adams told me the guy was a complete pest, following his team around to find out where they were looking, what they might know. Even went so far as to hang out while they were getting their samples. Adams almost choked telling me that the guy said he was a geology enthusiast. Always collected rocks as a kid."

Ted gave her an evaluating look. "If anyone was more fascinated with the outcome of Adams study, it was LaBelle."

"Well, that might explain why he wanted to know what Adams had learned. He seemed pretty eager to get this land," Christine said. "Turns out, there's no oil here after all."

"See, but that's just the thing," he pointed out, holding his empty wine glass up to Christine. She held the wine bottle out, showing him it was empty. Not a drop of wine was left, but his story seemed bottomless, and would have to be told without it.

"Right after Adams left, LaBelle doubled his efforts to sell the land in his industrial park. Put other sections up for sale too. You should see the glossy brochures he had printed up. I was sure he was going to hire an airplane to paper the countryside with them. Ruthie went with her sister when LaBelle conducted 'opportunity seminars' in Fargo and Minneapolis, pushing investors to pay him top dollar for parcels that he knew were visited by Adams team."

"That's good old-fashion speculation, wouldn't you say?"

"I'd say."

"And you said that he seemed even more eager to sell once Adams disappeared?"

"Well, yes. Maybe he thought the report he was hoping for was about ready to break. So he'd better milk the advance buzz for all it was worth. Or get the cash he needed to be able to acquire more," Ted said.

"Maybe he was hoping I'd be stupid enough to turn my land over to him, even to just get the commissions off of flipping it over to someone else. I don't know. It seems suspicious that Adams disappears, then he ramps into high gear," she said.

"I see where you're going with this," Ted pointed out. "I'm an old cop, so you don't have to connect the dots. LaBelle is well known around here, and not everyone has the best opinion of the guy. He can be pushy, no doubt, but he's harmless. I'm sure he had nothing to do with Adams's disappearance. The guy probably just got lost in the white-out, maybe got off track, slid off the road somewhere."

"If that was all it was, they would've found his car long ago," she said. "Yes, there's remote country out here, and some roads don't see too many travelers, but eventually another person comes by. If it was as simple as a guy driving off the road in a snowstorm, he'd have turned up by spring, at the latest. From what you tell me about Adams, he's also not the kind of guy who would've decided not to go home after all, you know, end it all here. He didn't sound depressed. Though he wasn't sure what he might encounter in retirement, he sounded like he was looking forward to at least weekends with his wife, right?"

"You've spent a lot of time around cops, haven't you?" Ted said.

"More than I'd like to at times, " she admitted. "To continue," she said. "The guy's a geologist. He's sent out to collect samples, map the countryside. I'm guessing he would've had a lot of high-tech gadgets to help him specifically identify where he was at any given time. Even phones have navigational devices. Why wouldn't anyone have tried to locate him via his phone?"

"Yeah, he had a lot of gear," Ted said. "He showed me some of his toys. I asked him if they had a setting for locating lunker bluegills. I admit," Ted said warily. "Things look suspicious."

"Not so much regarding his disappearance," he went on, "But why no one has been able to locate him yet. But, as I said, Carlson County took over pretty much right away. Then I retired."

Christine said nothing while she considered everything Ted told her.

"So why are you sitting there," Ted said, "stewing?"

"I'm not convinced everything was done that could have been done," Christine said. "To find the guy."

"So what? Are you accusing me of not doing my job?" Ted said. "Is that's what is on your mind?"

Christine paused again. She'd come to respect Ted for everything he'd done. But she did have questions. She wished Arvo would at least fill in some of the gaps. "I know that things are slow out here, I know you've retired and—"

"—washed my hands of this sordid mess?" Ted said.

"—and moved on," she said, trying to sound like she meant it. "Look, I'm not the best example when it comes keeping my work and private life separate. I'm not sure I even had a private life, until now. I have no idea how I'll handle retirement, when that day comes."

"Probably you'll be one of those people who works until she drops dead," Ted said.

"Maybe. Who knows. I was hoping to come out here and see how I'd manage a life without work," she said.

"So far, it seems like you're right back in it," he said.

"Well, it's a little difficult avoiding it when I wind up in the middle of a crime scene, and have a cop in my life 24-7," she said, exasperated.

"*Retired* cop," he stressed. "And who says it's a crime scene?"

Christine's phone chimed from inside the house just as Ted's phone went off. Both hurried to their respective devices.

"Arvo," Christine said without allowing the detective to announce himself.

"You sound actually happy to hear from me," he said.

Christine watched as Ted came inside and went to the room off the main living area. She thought she heard him switch on something.

"Spill it," she said. "What do you know?"

"They found your guy," he said. "In case you hadn't heard."

She heard the television news from the next room, and ran to watch the station Ted had tuned in. "Ruthie told me," he said, pointing to the phone.

They watched together, each with a cell phone in hand, still carrying on their separate conversations. Christine pressed her phone hard to one ear, plugging her other ear to be able to hear Arvo over the sound of the television set and Ted's conversation with Ruthie.

"Do you have any details? All I'm seeing is a bunch of cops and investigators, swarming around in the dark. Wait a minute, Ted's talking to me."

"Ruthie says a farmer found him on some land at the other side of Carlson County. Just reported on the Fargo news," Ted said, telling her exactly what they were watching scroll across the bottom of the screen, a repetition of what the reporter was saying. She was transfixed by the pictures, but they weren't telling her anything.

Adams rented truck was seen in the footage. It had been found in a heavily wooded section of hunting land near a farmer's field in remote Carlson County. The front of the pickup was submerged in a small creek.

"Authorities say the death of the renowned geologist is under investigation, neither confirming nor denying whether the man's death is suspicious. Earlier today his wife, Lisa Adams, arrived in Fargo." Though Christine wanted to see the footage of Lisa Adams, she knew it would have to wait. She left Ted to his conversation with Ruthie and the amplification of the sensational news on the television and walked outside to hear more about what Arvo knew.

"Were you able to learn anything?" she asked.

"My vacation was nice," he pointed out. "Jade says hi," he added.

"Arvo, come on. You know something, don't you?"

"Well, I didn't until just now. I'm not familiar with that part of the country, but something isn't exactly lining up. I learned this morning that they'd located the guy, where is it, the far western edge of Carlson County, right?"

"That's right. I saw that bit of news on the television."

"Carlson County told me," he paused a moment and she could here the rustle of papers, "that they'd initially detected his cell phone signal in that area, on the day after he was reported missing, but didn't locate him."

"I heard there'd been a blizzard out here. Pretty much shut everything down," she said.

"Yeah. That's what they told me. They had to put the search on hold because conditions were even too bad for them," he said. "They did have access to a helicopter but it was too dangerous to search from the air, and they were unlikely to spot anything anyway."

"Wait, you said initially detected his cell phone signal. What did you mean by that," she asked.

"They got ready to conduct a more exhaustive search a few days later, and got help locating his cell phone signal again," he said. "But when they located it, the found it in the opposite side of the county," Arvo said. "Miles away from where they'd first located it, and as it turns out, miles away from where they just today located what appears to be Adams's body."

Christine was thunderstruck. "Wait. Are you saying that the cell phone moved? I don't quite get that."

"That's right," Arvo said.

"What did the cops make of the cell phone location moving?" Christine said.

"They told me they figured that there'd been a mistake with their first reading. Maybe the storm knocked out some towers, and they got a misleading reference point the first time around. So when they picked up the search, the looked in the second area, which is obviously not where the guy was." Arvo said.

"And do you know where the second location was? Where they didn't wind up locating the guy?"

"Exactly the spot where you are, right now," he said. "They came back and searched every inch of the property. Didn't your friend, the retired cop, tell you about that?"

Ted was still inside the house, staring at the television set, transfixed, apparently, by the news of the discovery.

"Let me guess by your silence that the guy's there with you now. And that he didn't tell you that," Arvo said.

"And," Christine said, her heart about ready to leap out of her chest, "You can guess I'm not going to ask him about it now. What the hell?"

"Call me," Arvo said. "Later. After this ex-cop is gone."

She could hear his worried tone. "Yeah. Yeah, I will," she said, hanging up. She paced outside her house, waiting for Ted's call to end. She willed herself to get a grip, her mind racing, trying to come up with plausible excuses for Ted not to have told her that another thorough search had been made of her property, one he'd mentioned nothing about.

Ted came outside and saw her standing there watching him. "Wow, amazing that they finally found him, wouldn't you say?"

She smiled wanly. "I guess his wife will get the answers she came to get," she said.

"Who was that you were talking to?" he said, betraying no change from the same friendly guy he'd been all night long.

"Arvo," she said, partly in warning, not feeling the need to hide it. Still, she didn't want to let on that they'd already had a conversation about her suspicions, that she'd in fact sent him sniffing around. "Today's news about Adams hit the big time down there too. He'd heard the guy had been staying at my place before he went missing. Some kind of weird office humor, was calling to quiz me about my latest victim." She faked another smile. "Christine's trail of bad relationships continues."

"Well," he said, "I hope you dished it back at him. What a wise guy."

"Yeah," she said.

"I better be getting home. It's late," he said, "Though Ruthie will probably want to keep me up half the night with gossip. The town's going to be buzzing about this, no doubt. Well at least we know it's over now. The guy's been found, and it was the sad end we feared. Hopefully they can put the rest of this oil business to rest now."

He drove off without further comment, and once he was finally away, Christine quickly switched on her alarm system, securing her premises, and preparing for the worst. Her heart sank at the thought that the one person she'd finally felt safe to trust, could not longer be trusted. She glanced out her windows, the sky finally black, the stars blotted out by a thick layer of clouds.

17

THE CLOCK STRUCK 11:00 P.M. This would have been the perfect time to connect with the pre-Jade Arvo. The thought of post-Jade Arvo at this hour did cause her some pause. But it was a Monday night, he'd been back in the office an entire day. She willed herself to believe it unlikely that the two of them would be together. Was she more envious of Arvo's or Jade's happiness? She didn't know. And at the moment she envied more the security they undoubtedly felt, which was entirely lacking given her situation.

He answered on the first ring.

"Just getting ready to call you," he said, "I'm still at the office."

That she felt immediately relieved left her wondering whether it was because Jade wasn't there, or that he'd been thinking of her.

She poured out everything she'd learned in the report and what Ted had told her, talking so quickly and without interruption she almost didn't take a breath. She kept watch out her kitchen window, ready to take action if she saw anyone coming up the drive. Her hot nerves were buckshot, though she knew her voice betrayed none of her panic. She wondered whether the one person who knew her best would admire her cool or see through the bravado.

"He said nothing about this more extensive investigation around the house?" Arvo said once she came to the end of what she needed to tell him.

"Nothing. Nothing at all."

"The Carlson County detectives told me that the local officer had been contacted. They got the key to the place from him, in fact. You didn't hear about this either?"

"No," Christine said, "But honestly, Arvo, it'd been so long since I came up here. I was occupied with my job last winter, through the spring. Even if Ted had called me about any of this, I might have ignored him and put it out of my mind." She had also been occupied with another significant occurrence of her life: the first relationship she'd had with a man, and in a very long time.

She remembered the previous winter, which had been one of the better ones in her life. She and Arvo were navigating the early stages of their relationship with each other. Not that things were perfect between them. Far from it. As the two had known only enmity with one another, neither of them recognized that the long combative period that preceded their brief time as lovers for what it was: a drawn-out courtship. Their driving passion for work created the one weak point of their antagonism, and once broached, each saw the other in a new light.

For Arvo, there was only one person who could have jolted him out of wasting his time on a bad woman—his ex-wife—and that was Christine, the only woman direct enough to read the riot act on Arvo and his flaws (and there were many).

Christine certainly didn't want or need the complication of a relationship with any man. Why she would up with the last person she'd ever think of as a suitable life partner—a guy who couldn't hang up a jacket to save his life—was very complicated indeed, so complicated that she still wasn't quite sure how it happened. When she went down the list of "presenting symptoms" as she characterized her emotional state at the time, there were a number of contributing factors.

They'd been working together on a stressful and heartbreaking investigation that had nearly resulted in the death of her young, vulnerable patient—a key witness in the case—a haunting and precocious young girl. Christine had gotten very close to the girl—who disappeared at a crucial point in the investigation. So Christine was feeling a little vulnerable herself, and one night a few drinks with Arvo led to a few more drinks which led both of them to a bedroom and tenderness that both sorely needed, but didn't know how to tap without the assistance of alcohol.

She sometimes thought of that point in her life as the rock bottom. She was vulnerable. He was there. It happened. Then it was over. Despite the fact that she was the one insisting that they remain open to other relationships, and he hadn't planned on winding up in bed with his ex-wife, but did, she didn't even blame him for the betrayal. Perhaps because she had expected they wouldn't last. Really, their relationship seemed like a weary repeat of her parents' own history. Her dad's infidelity. Her mother's inability to keep from finding everything and anything wrong with him. Destiny programmed into her to make her fail with men.

Still, as she listened to Arvo on the phone, she reminded herself that it was over, even when the tender feelings she had stuffed down deep inside of her seemed to emerge. Just talking to him, someone she knew well, that remnant of tenderness, made the loneliness both worse and better.

"The cell phone signal?" He'd repeated. "How is it *not* possible for law enforcement to look through the records one more time? They told me that there weren't any calls made from the phone after the guy left Lucid. Then, when they first trace it, they find it in the vicinity of the place where his body was just found."

"You said they thought maybe the storm had shut down some of the towers? Maybe sent confusing signals?"

"Or," he said, "something more suspicious is going on. Maybe the guy's been killed, his truck and body hidden where no one would find him—"

"And miles away from the route he'd take between Lucid and the Fargo airport—"

"Then," Arvo said, "How does the phone signal come from the location of his body, then a few days later, right there in Lucid, the other side of the county."

"Is it possible, if this is a murder, that someone went back for the phone, knowing how law enforcement would use it to try to locate Adams? The mistake of a moment of passion? Maybe take it somewhere else and throw them off the scent?" Christine said.

"I suppose that's possible. But they'd have to go back, in the middle of the blizzard, to get the phone out of the place where they dumped the body," Arvo said, "During a time when no one was out, with one possible exception."

Christine gulped. "Ted said he rode a snowmobile out here when reports that the guy was missing came in."

"Do you know whether that was before, or after the second signal was located?" Arvo said.

"I don't know. I think it was when he was first declared missing," she said. "And he never even mentioned this second search."

"So, we don't know if it was Ted who retrieved the cell phone from Adams's car. How far is it to the other side of the county?" Arvo asked.

"Twenty miles. No problem on a snowmobile."

"Jesus," Arvo swore. "You said that he left your place, right? Went back home?"

"Yeah," Christine said. "He's gone. For now."

"Maybe you should get out of there. You said that he read the report with you, right? He knows what's in there?" Arvo's voice took on heightened urgency.

"Yeah. But it doesn't make any sense. What on earth would his motive be for killing the guy? If that's what happened?" Nothing was making sense to Christine, even though her mind raced.

"Who knows? Might have been an accident," Arvo said, presenting the first of several scenarios. "Maybe someone else did it and the cop knew, or found out about it. It sounds like there were plenty of people up there with a vested interest in hearing what was in that report. Maybe someone got rough with him, he wound up dying, and they had to make quick work in hiding the body.

And a cop would know how people are traced by cell phones. Maybe he's protecting someone."

"Did Carlson County say anything about what happened with the second signal?" Christine asked. "Did they locate the phone or find anything out here?"

"No. No phone. Whoever turned it on again either switched it off or just knew the battery would eventually wear out. The GPS in those devices can be quite accurate, and his was one of the best, according to what Carlson County learned in looking at his records. They pretty much had pinpointed the location of his body, but didn't follow up, and only went back to the other location now."

"It sounds sloppy to me," Christine said. "Not following up in the other location."

"These things can happen," Arvo said.

"It wouldn't have happened in Mendota County," Christine said. Arvo wouldn't have let it happen. He was sloppy in almost every aspect of his life except for work.

"Well, thank you for your confidence in Mendota County," Arvo said. "But mistakes get made. Some on purpose, but I think this was an honest mistake in Carlson County. At a certain point, you have to move on to the next thing, and hope for a break later. They told me when Mrs. Adams called them to tell them she was coming to town, she was getting off her plane and coming straight to Carlson County. I won't go into the colorful language they used to describe her personality."

"Ted told me that Adams said she could be ferocious. Best in small doses with long breaks in between." Christine pointed out. Maybe not so different from her. "Still, the woman's husband is missing and given all the gear we would expect a respected geologist to have on his person, I can understand why she might be on a tear with Carlson County for not finding him sooner."

"True enough," Arvo said. "I'm familiar with that type of personality. Unstoppable."

Christine didn't hear either a resigned or accusatory tone in his voice. She knew he had held that kind of opinion of her.

"Anyway," he went on, "her impending arrival prompted the detectives to look through the cold case file again, and it was at that point that they noticed that the first signals came from a location they had not exhaustively searched. They found the guy without a problem. And were helped by the fact that a raging blizzard, other than Mrs. Adams I mean, wasn't keeping them from the actual location of the geologist."

"Crap," Christine said, hearing her low battery alarm go off. "My phone's dying."

"Christine, you need to get out of there," Arvo said. "Now that this case is open again—if there are more tracks to cover, you can be sure that the perpetrators will be out covering them."

Even though her heart was in her throat, Christine knew she needed to hold her ground. This was her father's home, her home. Now was not the time to run away. "I'll be fine," she said, trying to sound like she meant it. She knew her voice was unwavering, cool again, or so she thought.

Except to the detective. "Then I'm coming up there," he said. He sounded like he meant it.

"No, Arvo, really," she said. "I've been around enough investigations, been charged with managing casework for truly vulnerable people to know when someone needs protective custody." She'd seen the worst of the worst. Children who needed to be kept from their own parents.

"And you know how vulnerable people are the last to ask for help," he said. "Please, Christine, you need to be straight with me."

Arvo had also been around the at-risk. He knew how victims often came to the aid of their abusers. A victim's fears of turning in someone they should be able to trust, but couldn't and shouldn't trust, based on past experience, was the number one threat to the personal safety of society's most vulnerable people. Frankly they hadn't learned what trust meant, given the long experience of trust being violated. The loving relationships that should have been, but weren't. Fear took the place where trust had been. Those attuned to working with the at-risk, like Christine and Arvo, were highly perceptive in sorting out who needed the most help.

"I am being straight with you. No one has even so much as laid a finger on me." Except, as she recalled, LaBelle. "Really, I've come across a couple of small town blowhards. That's about it. Probably this whole business will blow over, and it'll turn out that Adams actually just left his cell phone behind and basically just got lost in a blizzard. End of story."

"You don't really sound convinced of the story you're trying to sell me," Arvo said. "A world famous geologist, a guy who planned to retire in the mountains of West Virginia, seems like he'd know his way around the back country of Western Minnesota, even during a blizzard."

"Really. I can take care of myself. I don't need your help, Arvo." She massaged her fear into a persuasive ire to ward him off. It was ridiculous, really, to get this worked up.

"Well then why are you calling me?" he said, "Asking for help."

"In tracking down case details, Arvo," she said, trying to reassure him. "In case you forgot."

"Right, Ivory," he said. Dead air passed between them. Christine's phone battery beeped again.

"Get that phone charged up, Ivory," he commanded. "Expect a call from me in the morning. I don't care what you say. I'm keeping tabs on you."

The phone died before she could attempt another hollow reassurance, that she was fine and was going to be fine. She was relieved she didn't have to try and come up with something that would convince him when she couldn't' quite convince herself.

She glanced out her windows and saw a car headed her way on the county road. She held her breath as it came closer to her driveway, but it did, indeed, do what most cars did on the country road. It stayed on the county road, heading north and passing out of her view. A second passed by a few minutes later. The bars emptying out for the night. Fishermen heading back to their cabins and campsites to turn in early, planning on rising in the early hours.

"Foolish woman," she said to herself, having tapped out her nerves relating everything to Arvo. "Getting worked up over nothing." She willed herself away from the window and went through the story she had just told Arvo, the one where a world-famous geologist, searching for oil in remote areas of western Minnesota, accidentally gets lost on the way to the Fargo airport and manages to die, purely accidentally, but just before releasing a much anticipated final report.

Yep. Not entirely believable as an accident.

She then reminded herself that she had not wanted to get involved in the case. She had come out to peaceful, bucolic Lucid to take care of her dad's place, and get it ready for a quick sale, not really caring who might be interested in a quick buy. Even if it was slimy Greg LaBelle, a guy who had made an advance the week he was supposed to marry someone else.

Yep. No problem there. She'd be calling him first thing in the morning, to tell him he could have the place, at his price.

Not.

She sat at her kitchen table, drumming her fingers. Inactivity was the worst thing for her OCD, particularly when she was whipped up. And she'd already organized and categorized the contents of the pole barn, quickly filling in the gaps once she saw what Ted had returned. He had returned almost everything she'd identified as missing. The few remaining items she couldn't locate would have likely required replacement. It was a wash.

The house was also similarly reorganized, with not much more than a few hours of laundry to address the rest.

She flipped open her appointment book, an activity that usually helped calm her. Nothing was better than seeing page after page jammed with meetings, appointments, court dates, and sometimes multiple bookings over the same time period. She of course kept an online calendar, but she loved the sight of her handwritten notes, in ink.

The to-do lists that ran down the right hand columns were her pride and joy. To an ordinary person, so many tasks would have spelled either procrastination or doom. But Christine Ivory delighted in having a mountain of activity to work her way through. She assembled each day of her life like a champion puzzle enthusiast, expertly fitting tasks together in the thousand-piece jigsaw of a bustling life.

But the pages for the foreseeable future were blank. Every hour was empty, her calendar wide-open, all the pressing tasks completed before heading to Lucid. She'd seen everyone who needed seeing and cancelled her long list of regularly scheduled appointments—with her stylist, her manicurist, the unnecessary maid service. Arvo had ridiculed her for having a maid service when Christine was a meticulous housekeeper, in no need of even an occasional deep clean.

"What, Ivory?" he'd said when he'd heard of the maid, "Are you asking them to grade your work or something?"

"They help keep me on track," she said, which she knew sounded ridiculous. But even she knew that it was pointless to hire someone to tidy up the unused condominium of a neat freak.

She left her calendar open to the present date and tapped her pen against it. She needed to schedule like Arvo needed a drink. Just one appointment to give her a focus. She arrived on a candidate, thinking herself brilliant, and wondering how she hadn't thought of it hours earlier.

Greg LaBelle. She wanted information from him, and he wanted a quick sale from her. Both needs could be fitted together, not perfectly, but she'd make them work. She listed one task on the next date. Call LaBelle. She penciled in a block of time for the following evening. Dinner meeting with LaBelle.

She'd always faced her fears head-on, fitting them in with her dry-cleaning and facials, as if they could be handled best by those with professional cleaning credentials. But taking action was always better than doing nothing, and the best way to take action was by appointment. With that issue resolved, she walked through her house, closing every blind, and cocooning herself in the side room where the television set blared the late-night news. She muted the sound and settled in for another few pages of Harold Robbins, unaware that another car was approaching her driveway, this one with no intention of passing by. It pulled up just short of her driveway, and idled there for a few moments before making a U-turn to head back to town.

18

ABOUT FIFTEEN MINUTES BEFORE HER scheduled to-do of the next day, Christine's phone rang. LaBelle Realty. She rechecked her appointment book to note that his timing was prescient. Still she thought of letting the call go to voicemail. She wanted to control the timing, not him, but realized the advantage of not letting on to her plans lay in her answering the call. She checked the item off her list, closed her appointment book, and answered the phone.

"It's Greg," he said, "Greg LaBelle."

"Yes," she said. "Good morning."

"I was hoping you'd be interested in meeting me for dinner," he said. "You probably haven't had a decent meal since you arrived here."

She checked that task off her list.

"Is this a business dinner?" she asked, warning him off with just the right tone of annoyance in her voice.

"Let's just say it's personal, and if you want to talk business, of course I'm all ears," he offered. "Whichever works best for you. Those of us in the real estate business pride ourselves on good customer relations, and good food is always the best way to keep customers happy. My treat."

"I'm open to dinner," she said, not alluding to her objectives. "Where did you have in mind? I've been away so long I'm don't know where people dine out these days."

He mentioned a resort restaurant a few towns over, offering to pick her up at seven and bring her there. She said she preferred driving herself, telling him she had a few errands to run and would meet him there.

"The food is great, but I'll warn you the crowd is casual," he said to her, "Still, your jeans and t-shirt will look like cocktail dress to these folks."

She was familiar with the place he suggested. The restaurant was located in a century-old resort, a destination for many high-end vacationers staying in western Minnesota. Her dad had taken her to the restaurant on special occasions, and she knew the food was good, but the crowd could be rowdy, especially on a hot summer night. It was the type of place where a well-known local from a few towns over could blend in, especially when it was the height of summer vacation season and the place was packed with city-folk "roughing it" in a four-star resort, complete with a championship golf course and whirlpool suites.

With the time set, all she had to do was get through the long day. Arvo called a few hours later and she didn't betray her plans to him, ending the call but not until she promised him she'd call back later. He was still digging for information about the investigation.

"They aren't saying it in the news, but it is being investigated as a homicide. Given the state the body was in when they found it, it will take time to determine the exact cause of death. But it isn't an accident. A printer cable was wrapped around the guy's neck."

Now it was serious.

"You know what this means," Arvo said.

"Of course I do," she said firmly. She hoped he didn't hear the sound of her heart pounding through the phone. Stay calm, she told herself. "Do you know if they found his computer?" she said. "Other copies of the report?"

"Nothing was found with him other than his personal luggage. That's what I'm being told," Arvo said. "Their patience with me is running thin, I should tell you. They want to know why a Minneapolis area cop is interested in a western Minnesota investigation."

"You're smart Arvo. You'll think of a way to explain why you're interested," she said neutrally. She wanted him to keep the pressure on and make sure he was in the loop to receive updates, before they were given to the press.

"Obviously it can't be because I'm worried about you being at the location where the guy was staying before he was murdered. And that you have the only known copy of a report everyone was dying to read. And that you have an ex-cop you can't entirely trust as your first line of defense," he said in that irritated tone in his voice only she could bring on: her trigger pressed too hard on the cords of his aging bass. He cleared his throat.

He wouldn't hang up until she promised to call him later, and to immediately alert him if she sensed a change in threat. She remained resolute in not telling him of her plans to meet LaBelle. He would have put a stop to it. Arvo had already classified the man as a person of interest. But then, he would have classified almost everyone in Lucid the same way.

She turned the television cart so that the TV could be viewed in the dining room, and went about her business. She caught her first, brief glimpse of Lisa Adams, surrounded by reporters and thought she looked like what a retiring school principal should look like, though she stopped herself. She'd worked with all kinds of school principals over the years, and they came in all shapes, sizes and colors.

Lisa appeared to be a mountain of a woman, and every aspect of her appearance was enlarged, from the curly long hair that was barely restrained by her wide-brimmed straw hat, to her Rubenesque body that sent bulges in every direction, an abundant female territory for Adams' personal exploration. Her bosom was concealed under a flowing, floral dress. Even the glimpses she had of the woman, who towered over reporters, did not prepare her for the real person who turned up at her door an hour before Christine needed to leave to dine with LaBelle.

LISA ADAMS WAS THE TALLEST WOMAN Christine had ever met—her wide-brimmed hat brushing the top of the doorframe, and though she had to be close to two hundred and fifty pounds, she was the most radiant woman Christine had ever seen.

"Are you going to gape at me all day, Ms. Ivory," she finally asked. "Or are you going to invite me inside your home?"

The answer was obvious. Christine let her inside and closed the door.

19

CHRISTINE GLANCED OUT HER KITCHEN WINDOW, then turned to look again at her guest on one of her kitchen chairs.

"You noticed," she asked, "that I have no vehicle with me?"

"Yes," Christine said. "How did you get here?"

"I walked from town," she said. "I had the taxi drop me off just up the road. My husband told me he'd walked to and from town on many occasions. I thought I'd make my way here quickly before anyone noticed."

Christine wondered how a woman the size of Mrs. Adams could walk anywhere without being noticed. How she even managed to walk any distance without a lot of effort. But Mrs. Adams didn't seem the least bit flushed or out of breath. She removed her straw hat and laid it on Christine's table. She ran a hand through her unleashed curls and opened up a compact to adjust her lipstick, flicked a few hair strands free from her eyelashes, then clicked the compact shut and returned it to her purse.

"Is it just me?" Lisa said. "Or is law enforcement completely incompetent in this state?"

Christine opened her mouth, but Lisa stopped her.

"No. Don't answer. Why does it matter? It's not going to bring him back. Would you mind showing me around your home?" she asked.

"Certainly, but first let me say—"

"—you're sorry?"

"Yes—"

"—Don't bother expressing your sympathies," Lisa said, interrupting her again. "You don't know the man. I don't know you.

There's no need to bother with empty formalities." She waved off the social customs as if they were annoying black flies buzzing around her head. "I've just learned I'm a widow. And I never much cared for hollow customs—like condolences, Christmas caroling, greeting cards for every occasion. It's not your role to be the sympathetic friend. Not that I have any other people in my life that fall into that category."

"Do you mean you have no friends?" It sounded like Lisa Adams preferred blunt directness, a relief to Christine. "And I didn't mean that as an insult—"

"—an observation? Ah," Lisa Adams said. "Now we understand each other. I'm guessing you perhaps approach the people in your life the same way I do?"

"By steamroller?" Christine said.

"Yes. Something like that," she said, standing up once again, the stubborn expression on her face unchanged. "Well. Show me around. Oh, wait, I left something outside." Lisa Adams opened Christine's front door and retrieved a battered, rolling suitcase. "My husband's. I never traveled, so I had to use an old one of his when I came out here. He told me there were two bedrooms in this house? Will you show me the one you aren't using?"

Without comment or protest, Christine showed the widow to her father's old bedroom, the one Adams had used while he rented the place. "This will do perfectly. I think I'll find comfort and rest in the bed where my husband last slept."

"I'm happy to offer it to you," she said, even though she hadn't offered so much as a glass of water to the widow. It didn't matter. She was very sincere when she told the widow she could stay as long as she liked.

"Oh, well, you'll want me to leave sooner than you think. Steve always told me I was like that rich, delicious meal that one looked forward too all year, then consumed too quickly, having many more helpings than one required. Always a bellyache afterward and a promise to never indulge in quite that manner the next time. He always needed a long period of anticipation before he was ready for me again. But the whole cycle never changed. It was an addiction, for both of us, really."

Christine couldn't help but to ask. "You loved each other, didn't you?" She would never have ventured such a personal question with any other person. But she guessed that Lisa Adams wanted to be asked.

"Oh. Yes." One tear fell out of each eye. She dabbed her eyes with the edge of her sleeve. Those two tears expressed the deep-down grief she concealed with her brusque attitude. "We did love each other, that was true." She sat on the bed and bowed her head a few moments.

"Oh," Christine said remembering her appointment. "I have an engagement this evening and some errands to run beforehand. Please, feel free to go anywhere you like on the property. There are a few things in the fridge. Help yourself. I'm sorry that I have to leave even though you've just arrived."

"I expect no one will bother to come looking for me here. I had that retired police officer—"

"Ted Nelson?"

"Yes. My husband spoke well of him. I had Officer Nelson make arrangements for me. As far as everyone knows, I'm staying in Pelican Falls. Once I saw the cameras set up outside the hotel, waiting to pounce on me, I hired a cab and got myself driven out here," Mrs. Adams said. "It was an impulse," she said. "Don't worry, I won't stay forever. I didn't even know until the moment I arrived that I needed to stay here," she added. "I'm sorry you have a helpless widow on your hands."

"Let's just say you don't seem very helpless. You're just recalibrating," she offered.

Lisa laughed. "That's *exactly* how my husband would've put it. Recalibrating. He must've left something of himself in this place."

"In fact, he did," Christine said, getting Adams parka out of the cabinet and handing it to her.

"My word," Lisa said. "How on earth would he have left his coat behind?"

Christine didn't want to mention what she'd learned from Arvo. That most likely it wasn't by his choice that the jacket was left behind. If all Lisa Adams was going on, in regards to her husband's death, was what the media reported, then she would not know that it was being investigated as a homicide. Christine didn't bring up the other significant item left behind. She didn't have time to go into the level of detail needed, and find out what, if anything, Lisa Adams knew about the results of her husband's study.

"Please. Make yourself at home."

"Thank you, Ms. Ivory. I would apologize for barging in on you, but frankly I'm not in the best mood. Did you know I can't even begin to make funeral arrangements or plan to get my husband back to West Virginia until they've finished the autopsy?"

Christine knew very well how these things went.

"My word. I've felt stuck in place for months, and now it seems I have to wait even longer," she said. "I'm not used to waiting for other people to take action. I can't stand it."

"I think, on that subject, you and I have a lot in common." She wanted to stay longer and speak to the woman. She realized that even someone as self-sufficient as Mrs. Adams had the same needs as many of her patients. It struck her that in accepting Mrs. Adams into her home, she was in many ways back in a role she'd recently left. That of a medical professional assisting victims of crimes.

"I'm very sorry to have to leave you on your own," Christine said, having briefly explained her occupation, and what she might be able to offer the widow. Mrs. Adams surprised her by letting down her guard, admitting that she was sure she'd be fine, but looking forward to more conversation with Christine.

"I'll be honest," Christine said as she was getting ready to head out. "You're the best company I've had since I came up here. It's probably my fault—I don't always make the best first impression, but clearly," she added, "You don't either."

Lisa oversized laugh matched her physique. "You seem to understand me perfectly," she added wheezing with her last breath of laughter. "Bravo. A woman who speaks her mind. How refreshing after a lifetime of having people approach me on tip toe."

"I can imagine you were quite formidable in the Charleston School District," Christine said. She must have cut quite the figure striding through schoolrooms, towering over not only the students, but everyone in the faculty and staff.

"I'm pleased to report that for many years running, my school, Thomas Jefferson High, had the best test scores in the state and among the highest graduation levels."

The women exchanged a few more remarks about their similar attitude towards their careers, and life, and Christine was reluctant to break away from her new friend. She made another musing remark. "You realize, of course, that your husband brought us together. With his death."

Lisa Adams wiped away a tear or two ("from the laughs you given me"), and said, "As hard as my husband's death is to take, particularly given all the whoopla, I think I may have landed, temporarily, in the exact place where I needed to be. I usually hate being out in the country. Really couldn't stand the thought of spending a lot of time in his retirement place. All of my social life was connected to my work. I'm not really sure how those relationships will transition to retirement, if at all. But maybe it was the company that kept me tied to Charleston. Now that that's gone, I may wind up moving to Snowshoe. See how my other half lived. Start fresh."

"I'm finding myself hobbled the same way, even though my leave is temporary. It's really throwing me off my game. Starting fresh was what I'd hoped to do by coming out here."

"Well, it seems my husband's death has changed both our lives." She put one of her huge hands on Christine's. "I don't want to keep you any longer. I'm sure there'll be plenty of time for us to talk later."

"I'm looking forward to it," Christine said.

Lisa Adams gave Christine's dinner dress the once over. "My," she said, "you know a thing or two about style. I hope whoever you're meeting is going to make tonight worth your while."

Christine had dressed herself in a simple white cotton dress, her naturally wavy short brown hair left to curl where it liked.

"You look like a vision from a Bergman film."

Christine blushed, feeling even more flattered knowing the compliments were coming from someone who wanted nothing from her but her friendship. She thought of explaining the security system, but decided not to bother. She'd be back in plenty of time to arm it later. Mrs. Adams wasn't the one with the oversensitive nerves, anyway. She'd most likely scare the daylights out of any possible intruder.

Lisa spotted the Harold Robbins' novel, asking Christine if she minded whether she read it. "I haven't seen this since back in my college days," she said. "I wonder how risqué it seems these days."

"Go ahead," Christine said, pointing out the other available reading material on her nightstand.

"Oh, my, no thank you," Lisa said. "This will do. Something to really take my mind off the events of the past few days. Nothing like good old fashioned smut for that." She settled in for a read, using her husband's parka as a cushion, and someone managing to curl up her robust figure on the small bed where her husband last slept. Precious and Semi-Precious found comfortable perches on her amply padded thighs. Before departing for the evening, Christine poured her houseguest a glass of white wine and left the bottle in her bedroom.

20

The parking lot at Serenity Lake Lodge was jammed, as one would expect on a beautiful summer evening in western Minnesota. Christine maneuvered her Volkswagen Passat between the oversized SUVs, nearly being broadsided by one driver hurrying through on her way to snag an open spot. She swore when she saw the distracted, blond female driver on her cellphone, obliviously paying no attention to her, nor anyone else. She hated when women drivers drove poorly. They made all women drivers look bad.

With the number of families enjoying the resort, the woman could have easily run down a toddler. As it was, she almost crashed into a determined and somewhat frazzled social worker on holiday, delaying her from her dinner with a possible murder suspect. Of course, this was only the theory of two former coworkers, only one of whom was qualified to have such an opinion, and he was hundreds of miles away, back in his own jurisdiction, likely enjoying a quiet dinner with his beautiful, uncomplicated girlfriend, having completely put obsessive, combative Christine Ivory, and all of her problems, out of his mind.

Christine stepped out of her car, and saw the woman who had just nearly killed her exiting her SUV. She was about to walk over to the woman to give her a piece of her mind when a voice called from nearby.

"Chrissy," Greg LaBelle said. "Sorry I'm late. I had something to tie up in Lucid. I hope you haven't been here long."

It was obvious she had just arrived, but she merely commented that her errands had kept her longer than she thought they would.

She watched the bad driver totter off on extremely high heels, which Christine dismissed as the wrong color given her tight mini dress.

"You look great," LaBelle said, lingering on parts of her physique a more polite man should not be caught lingering on.

He looked about how he'd looked the previous day. Smarmy. Overweight. Overtanned.

They arrived at their reserved table on the deck, which looked out onto Serenity Lake. The tiny deck tables were squeezed together, and he pulled his chair closer to her than was necessary.

The lake was crowded with pleasure boats, and the lodge patio packed with dinner guests showing lots of summer skin.

"We used to keep a boat here," LaBelle pointed out. "But we never used it, so I sold it last year to a guy from Minneapolis. Made a nice profit on it. I picked it up from an auction just the year before back. The recession, believe it or not, has been great for business."

"Yes," Christine commented, "if you can make a buck off of someone else's misfortune, why not?"

The waitress dropped by with menus and a hurricane candle, and the moment their candle was set down, it blew out. "Well, we can't have that," LaBelle said, quickly retrieving a lighter from his pocket and relighting it. "There," he said, pushing the candle closer to Christine. "The flame casts a pretty light on that hot white dress of yours."

"How's Meridee?" Christine asked. "Wasn't she coming tonight?"

"Meridee gets bored with my affairs," he said. "Business and personal." His eyes lingered again a fraction too long where they shouldn't, before locking on Christine's eyes. He smiled. "Meridee's learned to accept that she has a hard-working businessman for a husband, and that late hours and unexpected absences are the rule. She's rewarded handsomely for her efforts," he said.

"So she's the happy homemaker?" Christine said.

"Something like that," he said. "I can see that you don't think too much of the arrangement."

"It's really not an area where I care to pass judgment," Christine said. "Having never actively pursued nor been offered such a role."

"So you wouldn't ever see yourself in the role of a happy homemaker?" he asked, putting a hand on top of hers. "Not something that a career girl like you could handle?"

"It's not that I couldn't handle it," she said, sliding her hand away as quickly as I could. "But I'm used to being an independent woman, making all of my own decisions, not having to be dependent on someone else."

"I see," he said. "But you're still fine with me footing tonight's bill," he said, "Living off the benefit of your dad's wise investments. You didn't do much to earn yourself the fine spread your dad acquired. Nice that you can come into such a fortune."

Here came his angle. Christine knew she would have to put up with him a bit longer. She was doing everything she could not to hold her nose in disgust.

"I'll admit," she said, "The man did well, and I have him to thank for whatever I benefit from his acquisitions."

"Anyone can see you're more of a city girl. You could sell his place and get yourself a condominium at a vacation destination more your style. New York City. San Francisco."

The waitress dropped off their drink order and asked whether they were ready to order dinner yet. Christine's stomach turned at the idea of dining with LaBelle. "Not quite yet," she said.

"Yes, we'd like to linger over our drinks. Enjoy the evening." The waitress left. "Why hurry," he said, "Unless you'd prefer a more intimate spot, maybe out of the sun to protect that lovely skin. Really, you look like one of those expensive porcelain dolls my wife collects and keeps locked inside her glass cabinets.

Couldn't quite get her fascination with them until now." He smiled, his eye appraising her value in a collection.

Christine didn't know how she was going to be able to keep her stomach contents down, her interest in any conversation with him up. Still, even in his attempts to flatter her, which came off so badly that even the waitress rolled her eyes when she heard his lines in passing, there wasn't a malevolent edge. He seemed cartoonish.

"You're right," she said, finding an area where she could agree with him, and using that as a conversation sustainer. "This isn't really my thing. No sportsman husband to keep entertained, no kids who need fresh country air. Leisure doesn't really help me much."

"The last time we spoke you didn't seem terribly interested in selling."

"I'm still not," she said. "But of course, long term, I have to figure out what to do with the Lucid property."

"Well," he said, "You could still just turn it over to me. Get it off your hands."

"It would help to know whether or not there's oil under the property," she said. "Wouldn't it? I mean, without that question answered, any sale is in limbo, since the property can't be accurately valued."

"That shouldn't stop you from an immediate sale," he said. "That's the thing about land. The value can just as easily go down as up. Even with the oil issue in question, we're years away from value in that area. You sell now, get the value out of it as agricultural land (and there's a pretty penny there), and let's say there's not a drop of oil under there, you get the maximum profit you could have out of the place, and some other sucker is stuck with not terribly profitable farmland. Waiting is about the worst thing you could do."

"Unless of course it turns out there is oil," she said, "and the value skyrockets the moment a discovery is verified." She watched him closely. What did he actually know? Were money woes fueling his need to acquire her land in a pyramid scheme, and flip it to someone else quickly? Or was he still thinking an even larger profit was available?

He looked at her with cunning and hungry eyes. "And no one knows yet what the man found."

No one but Christine, Ted, and possibly the murderer, Christine thought. "Now that they found him, won't they find his reports with him?"

"Who knows?" LaBelle said. "That body and whatever remained with it have been out in the elements for quite some time. This environment isn't particularly friendly to delicate materials—computer hard drives, paper reports, geologist's bodies."

He looked at her again. "What would it take to get you to sell now? You would walk away from here with the certain value, rather than waiting for the whims of a market adjustment, which could go either way. That's the risk in waiting," he said. "Or maybe you like putting yourself at risk? Taking your father's carefully acquired estate and just risking the value of it by waiting longer?"

The waitress dropped by again, but LaBelle waved her off this time. "Why are you bothering with Lucid at all, Chrissy? Be sensible. I'm prepared to offer you the going rate for acreage and the buildings. On the spot. You could leave tonight, never come back. You don't have any family here any longer. Haven't we made you miserable with our small town ways?"

"Have you been trying to make me miserable?" she asked bluntly.

"Of course not. We've done our best to welcome you. You don't seem terribly interested in accepting what we have to offer," he said. "Beautiful country. Friendly people. I know I've always enjoyed your company and wished I could have had more." He leaned an elbow on her chair, invited himself into her personal space. "If you're going to stay, you could at least show us some affection."

She stood up, knocking her untouched drink into his lap. "I think I've had enough of your affection," she said, "though that's not what I'd call it." She tossed money onto the table. "And I won't have you paying for my entertainment here, though again, that's not what I'd call it."

"Well, now," he said, dabbing his lap where her drink had spilled. "What's gotten you so hot and bothered, when all I'm trying to show you is a good time?"

She ignored his question. "Let me be perfectly clear with you. I'm not selling the property now. If I decide to sell, at some point in the future, I won't be selling it to you. Further, if you ever set foot on my property again, without my permission, I will consider it trespassing and won't hesitate to use any legal law enforcement authority to keep you off my property."

"I take it you aren't staying for dinner?"

She shot him a hostile look, and threw another twenty dollars on the table. "That should cover your dry-cleaning."

"Women. You can't ever be satisfied, can you?" he said, shouting after her and brushing her money off the table.

She walked away shaking her head. She had let the irritation get the better of her, and she drove away thinking she might have been better off chatting with Lisa Adams rather than trying to play detective and get information from a sleazy operator like LaBelle. It sounded like the Carlson County Sheriff's Office, as inept as it had been up to this point, was finally getting things in hand. LaBelle clearly didn't know anything but was only out for the quickest buck he could make.

She hurried to her car, wanting to put as much distance between herself and the man as she could. It didn't take her more than a few miles to realize that she would not achieve what she'd hoped. She'd only gotten as far as a few miles away from Serenity Lake, when she saw his car, fast approaching hers from behind.

21

Christine's Passat was no match for LaBelle's high-powered SUV. The faster she drove on the curving, rolling roads of Carlson County, the closer he came. He wouldn't need to rear-end her, she knew. She just had to take a curve too fast and be thrown off the road. Would he go so far as to implicate himself by causing an accident? It would ruin him. But then he might be the man responsible for Adams's murder. Her heart raced but she kept focused, driving in the direction of a highway onramp. She'd be safer on the highway, and counted on the Interstate Highway Patrol to turn up when she needed them. She knew they ran extra patrols in the summer.

It was not her lucky day. Before she knew it, she was one exit away from the main Lucid exit, with not a Highway Patrol cop to be seen. She had, however, gotten ahead of him when a pair of semis blocked both lanes for the last mile, with LaBelle on the other side. She decided to play it safe and exited early, knowing she could take the back roads to her place, and get there well ahead of him. She didn't want Lisa Adams facing him alone, if indeed he planned to chase her all the way back there.

She pulled onto the frontage road and after only driving a block, found the road ahead closed. Beyond the barriers she saw an abandoned industrial park project, the huge signs that read "Coming Soon" now looking worn and filled with graffiti. As fast as she'd tried to get away from that smirking expression, there it was again in front of her, promising that LaBelle Industrial Center was the place to locate in Western Minnesota's burgeoning, oil boom future.

She turned into the unfinished parking lot, hoping there was a way to get around the piles of construction debris, and make her way quickly back onto the frontage road. Turning around and heading back onto the highway would only lead her back to LaBelle, and she needed all the time she had to get home to Lisa. The deep ruts in the dirt, left behind by heavy construction equipment, had been filled with water from snowmelt, and now they were a combination of muddy sinkholes and gravel mounds, miniature replicas of what the glaciers had left behind eons ago, before the accumulations of topsoil made the area more hospitable. Only one building actually appeared complete on the site: a trailer housing the complex's sales office.

Christine found tire tracks that led to the trailer offered better driving, even though the bumps continued to jar her, and her car's underbody scraped and banged against the rough ground. This was the one time in her life she wished she had an SUV. Her Jetta's tires spun out in the muddier areas, and ultimately became mired right as she came to the trailer.

What a nightmare, she thought as she struggled to get out of her car and make her way to the trailer. She found her way to the far side of it and then she saw a sporty new pick-up truck parked there, hidden from view until then. Like her vehicle, its wheels were caked with mud, but not stuck in the muck like she was. Maybe someone was inside who could help get her to her house, though she wondered why LaBelle would bother to have someone still managing sales for the obviously defunct and inaccessible industrial park.

She ran up the portable stairs and banged on the door.

A woman opened the door. She looked somewhat familiar to Christine, but she couldn't quite place her at first. A younger, wealthier version of Ruth. She wore a cheap-looking fur coat over her ample body and her overdone hair, nails, and makeup only made her look like she was trying too hard to appear elegant, Parisian.

"The nerve," the woman said. "Of course, I shouldn't be a bit surprised. She almost spat out the words. "He brought all of his women here. That is, when he couldn't bring them out to your dad's place."

It was LaBelle's wife, Meridee.

"It's not what you think, Meridee," Christine said, hating LaBelle enough to want to rat him out to her. But she didn't want to get into the middle of their marital mess. Still the idea that LaBelle might have been using her house as a trysting spot was too much.

"If what you're thinking is there's something between your husband and me, that is absolutely the last thing that would ever happen," she said, leaving it at that. The tone of her voice made it clear how much she despised the man.

"Oh, really," she said, giving Christine's sexy outfit a good long look. "I heard that you were seen with him down at Serenity Lodge. Oh, I have my sources. I know it's true, so don't bother telling me anything else. He sent you here, to meet him. There's no way it's anything else."

The unmistakable sound of another vehicle trying to make its way across the quagmire ended the conversation. In moments, they heard a vehicle door slam and someone approaching from the other side of the trailer.

"Meridee," LaBelle said with obvious surprise. "You're back?"

Meridee stood in stony silence, glaring at her husband as he looked back and forth between the two women.

"It's not what you think," he said.

"Funny, that's exactly what Chrissy just told me," Meridee said. "Now what exactly do you think I suspect? As I told Chrissy, I know both of you were together at the lodge."

Christine wanted to point out what really had happened. That Greg LaBelle had accosted her, and nearly tried to run her off the road. But clearly Meridee was doing a fine job of the heavy lifting.

"We were having a business meeting. That was all," he said.

"That you were going to continue here?" she said. "Oh, I know what kind of business you conduct here. What kind of business you've always conducted here."

Greg LaBelle walked towards the trailer, his hands positioned either to defend himself, or attempt to calm her. Christine began backing down the stairs.

"Just wait inside," LaBelle said to his wife. "I need to have a word with Chrissy."

"NO WAY," Meridee said. "I'm not going to let the two of you get your stories straight. I'm not leaving."

"Meri? Please?" LaBelle's forehead was dripping in sweat.

She wouldn't back off. Christine edged past LaBelle, who was too distracted with his wife's fury to notice.

"Did you think I didn't know?" Meridee went on. "About any of this? Your women? I've known for years? And to think you would take up with that skinny bitch outsider," she said. "My god. She's hardly even looks like a woman."

Christine wished she could mention that even when she'd hardly been a mere girl, LaBelle had been after her. But she thought the better of trying to get on Meridee's side in attacking her worthless, cheating husband.

"Meridee. No. You really need to calm down and get a grip."

"Get a grip? Are you kidding me? I'll tell you what I'm going to get a grip on. A divorce lawyer, that's what," she said. "I've had enough of your women, your failed schemes."

Christine had made it to the side of the trailer, out of their line of vision, and knew now was the time to hurry. Maybe she could back out, now that LaBelle was occupied, and head down the highway. The problem was that LaBelle's vehicle was blocking her way, still running.

Then it came to her. She'd do what others in town had done, when there'd been a need. It was her turn to do the borrowing.

She hopped inside LaBelle's truck, the stink of his cologne almost putting her back out, slipped it in gear, and backed out and around. By the time Meridee was done with her husband, which looked like it was not going to be anytime soon, she'd be ready to return his vehicle to him. How could he mind?

22

Moments later, she turned LaBelle's SUV onto her driveway, sped up and parked next to the closed pole-barn, hurrying inside her house to alarm her system. She didn't notice at first that her front door was unlocked and wide open.

"Lisa?" she called into the quiet house. No answer. The television was off. The Harold Robbins book lay open on the bed in the room where Lisa had installed herself, the kittens nowhere to be seen.

Now that was a trick. Many items had gone missing from the place—but how a 250-pound woman could have disappeared really took the cake.

Well maybe she just walked into town, Christine thought. She'd walked from there to her house. Somehow, though, Lisa didn't seem like the kind of person to walk away and leave a door open. She'd kept track of thousands of children over the years. She would know enough not to leave a door open behind her.

Christine glanced down her driveway, surprised not to see LaBelle or his wife there, but relieved. She walked the perimeter of the pole barn and found no sign of Lisa, anywhere. She listened to the still evening, and heard only the sound of the songbirds, the slight ruffling of prairie grasses releasing the shimmering heat of the day that had tensed low in the fields. Then she heard it. A low, slow moan of pain. It came from deep inside her pole barn of all places.

She opened the service door and stepped inside, flicking the light switch several times. *Damn*, she thought. *How did I not notice the lights weren't working?* She left the door open behind her and in moments, her eyes adjusted to the dark.

She heard the moaning once again, and saw that it was Lisa lying on the ground moaning, the worn out wooden ladder lying on the ground next to her.

"I think my leg is broken," she said, wincing in pain. "Came out to try and find the cats, thought I heard them mewing from the top shelf."

What happened was easily determined from the position and condition of the ladder. She'd climbed at least partway up, but fallen when a rung broke under her weight.

"But how did the service door get closed behind you?" Christine asked, helping the woman sit up.

Lisa shook her head.

"It wasn't you?" Christine asked. "Was someone else here?"

"Two people. An older woman. A heavy set young guy. Came out looking for you, asking to see the report you showed Ted." She panted between sentences. "I told them I didn't know what they were talking about."

Yes, Ruth had known very well the report she was referring to. Obviously Ted had mentioned what they'd found, and word had gotten quickly to around town. Clearly it was Ruth and Joey who'd come snooping around. Though why they would want to see the report didn't make any sense. There was no oil. What was the point of rereading the report, something neither of them would understand.

"They knew who I was," Lisa said. "Seen me on TV."

"When were they here?" Christine asked.

"An hour ago," she said. "I thought they'd gone. The door to the house. Hadn't closed. Cats got out. I came out here. Fell in the dark."

Christine heard footsteps running outside, and raced to the door. She caught a glimpse of someone outside just as he arrived ahead of her.

"Too late," Joey Dunn shouted before slamming the door in her face, keeping her from opening it with his massive strength.

"You can't stand there forever," she said. "Open it up before you cause even more trouble for yourself. Your mother. Why are you doing this, Joey?"

She heard him laughing. "Mom? Chrissy, thinks I'm causing you trouble, Mom. Am I?"

"What are you talking about, Joey?" It was Ruth. "Just hold tight, Joey, I'll be done in a minute."

"Ruth?" Christine said, banging on the door. "Let us out of here. There seems to be a misunderstanding. Can't we talk about this?"

Christine had learned techniques for ending a hostage crisis. Just try to keep a conversation going in any way possible.

"Misunderstanding? I doubt it. You've made yourself pretty clear from the moment you got here," Ruth said. "And apparently no one could convince you to do the right thing, meaning sell this place to LaBelle and leave immediately. We waited as long as we could for you to make the right decision."

"We?"

"For an educated girl, you sure aren't very smart," Ruthie said.

Joey laughed from a distance.

"You mean—you and Ted?"

"Ted has nothing to do with this. What do you think, we're idiots? We're going to alert the police department? Ted was useless anyway. He could never get that geologist to pass along what he'd learned. Doesn't Lucid deserve to know whether or not there was oil here? Before anyone else? And on this property? Ted's been busting his hump for years keeping things up here. Ted put all the effort into maintaining this place. That means it's as good as ours."

"Yours?"

"Look, we were willing to get you a fair price, but we deserved what it really could have been worth, that's what my brother-in-law, Greg, told us. But what is it really worth? Only the geologist knew and since Ted couldn't get the story from Adams—before it goes public—of course it was left to us to get it straight. Was there oil or not? Leave it to Joey to apply a little too much pressure trying to get the guy to give it up."

So Joey was the killer. "But there was no oil," Christine said.

"Yeah, Greg figured that out, after he had a look at the guy's computer. And of course you know that now too."

"So why is everyone after me to sell the place? Fast. There's no oil. We all know that."

Then she smelled the gasoline fumes.

"Only you, Joey, LaBelle, and I know that. There's still time to flip your place. Well, there was. Until today."

Christine could smell even stronger fumes and thought she heard the sound of liquid splashing against the door.

"If you had just come here, sold the place, and left, we'd all be fine. But you found the missing report. You learned the truth. Adams's body turned up. We can't risk it," Ruthie said, the sound of her voice growing faint.

Christine ran to the switch for the power garage door, but flipped the switch to no avail. *They cut the power.* The manual pull for the door was high above her head, out of reach except by ladder. The only one sat in pieces next to Lisa.

She heard the unmistakable sound of a car coming up her drive, spitting gravel and cracking black walnut fruits. It was probably Greg LaBelle, here to aid and abet his wife's sister in burning her and Lisa Adams alive. Maybe even Meridee was in on it.

She knew it would be pointless to cry out for help. That was until she heard an unexpected and unmistakable voice.

"Strange place to start a bonfire folks," he said. "Unless the owner has asked you to burn her barn down, which I doubt, but will happily leave you to it if you can tell me whether Christine Ivory as at home?"

23

"I'M HERE, ARVO" CHRISTINE SHOUTED as loudly as she could. "Inside. An injured woman is with me."

Arvo answered her only with grunts and groans, telling Christine that a struggle had broken out.

"He's a cop," she screamed for him, wondering if they'd already figured that out. She hoped he was armed, but then feared that at the same time. She heard steps, racing away from the pole barn. The sound of the first shot told her that someone was armed. She hoped it was him. And only him.

"Arvo!" She shouted his name again. It went unanswered. The flames were starting to reach under the doorway, aided by the flammable material conveniently placed, and not by accident, on the inside of the door.

"Holy shit," Christine said. "Can you move at all, Lisa?" she said.

"Probably only if I drag myself," the woman puffed. "There's a police officer outside already?" she asked.

"Yeah. Old friend of mine, but he sounds busy. I think we're going to have to get ourselves out of here, and fast."

Christine helped Lisa move as close to the big garage door as she could, pulling her as far away from the advancing flames as she could manage. She heard more gunshots outside, some of which hit the pole barn.

"Are you still okay in there, Christine?" Arvo yelled from somewhere nearby. "It's going to be a few minutes," he said.

"Oh, everything's fine, Arvo," Christine said, searching around the barn for some way to barricade herself and Lisa from the flames. "Why don't you just try and keep yourself from getting killed. We'll figure out how to get out of here."

Several more shots hit the corner of the barn. "They're taking cover by your house. I'm going to try and draw their fire away from the barn. Find something—a shovel, a hammer, whatever, and try to break your way out of there."

Christine searched for what he mentioned, then noticed something better. "Just stay away from the big door," she said.

He didn't answer. She could only hope he heard her. She jumped on the tractor and, for the first time in twenty years, fired it up. When it immediately stalled, she worried she might have flooded it. She hit the ignition again. It sputtered to life. She flipped it into gear and accelerated, hoping its top speed of thirty miles an hour would be enough to bring the door down. Before impact she apologized, "Sorry, Daddy," and ducked. The tractor crashed through.

She wanted to scream for victory, but really had no time to celebrate. She jumped off the tractor and ran back to pull Lisa Adams to safety. Then she spotted the best prize she could have hoped for: the welcome sight of Arvo, pressed against the side of her house. She ran to his side.

"Boy," Arvo said, seeing the flames rising on the side of the barn. "They sure are giving you a warm welcome here." He panted hard.

"Not so much," she said, "Are you okay?" She searched him for bullet wounds. She remembered the last time she'd seen him, injured and close to death. The last time she came so close to losing him.

"I'm okay," he said, his eyes holding hers a moment, flashing joy. "But how about you give me a proper Lucid welcome later, that is, without the bonfire," he said. "And the gunshots."

"Okay. But for now I need to get inside the house. Cell phone and maybe some back up fire for you," she said, catching him look at her a bit incredulous.

"Oh, I've had my firearm training," she said. "It's practically required out here. My dad was an excellent shot."

"Be my guest," he said, edging both of them around to the front door, while keeping a watch on Ruth and Joey, who were at the back of the house.

She hurried inside to where her father's guns had been stored in a bedroom gun safe. She opened the safe to find the guns, but no ammunition. "Crap!"

Then she remembered the last weapon of any kind, save a kitchen knife, would be in her closet. As usual, she'd preferred a different weapon, something on the slightly more stylish and unusual side. Her dad had laughed at her when she asked for it, but was very proud at his daughter's ability. Moments later she was armed, and rejoined Arvo outside.

"You know how to use that?" he said.

She nodded but kept her eyes trained on the corners of her house.

"You are a woman of surprises, Ivory," he said.

Shots came from opposite sides of the house and a moment later Joey jumped out closest to Arvo, pointing his rifle at them. Ruth stepped out from the other side and aimed directly at Christine, but a look of surprise came across Ruth's face before she could manage to pull her trigger.

Christine heard Joey cry out in pain, his gun silenced by a quick, accurate shot of Arvo's.

Ruth fell gasping, the look of surprise still on her face, an arrow through her ribs. Arvo quickly subdued Joey and cuffed him and Christine kept watch over Ruth with her crossbow while Arvo ran to the pole barn to help Lisa move further away from the fire.

Lucid's only police officer came screaming up to the house in his squad car, taking over for Arvo and Christine before the onslaught of a half-dozen squads and volunteer fire departments from neighboring towns, ambulances from the nearest hospitals and much of the Carlson County Sheriff's Department arrived like the calvary.

Lisa Adams was taken away to Pelican Falls, but not before Christine told her she would be there as soon as possible to make sure her new friend was being well cared for.

ONCE ALL THE NOISE HAD DIED DOWN, the suspects taken to the county for booking and detention, and the fire was out, Christine was able to learn that Greg LaBelle would not be pestering her anytime soon. Dent McCauley actually had been on his way to arrest LaBelle and confiscate more records from the Industrial Park Sales Office, and when he arrived, the husband and wife were still at it. Had Christine waited only a few minutes more, she would have seen LaBelle being hauled off in handcuffs.

Arvo explained more later. While looking into the geologist's disappearance, he and Carlson County realized that both were investigating another issue involving defrauded investors of a failed industrial park, just outside Lucid. Greg LaBelle's scheme had reach down to Minneapolis, and eventually to Somerset Hills.

"He'd been traveling everywhere trying to drum up support for an abandoned project. One of our Mendota County staff contributed to their investigation with a huge break in the case. Someone with expertise in tracking things down on the web.

"Kieran!" Christine asked.

"Who else?" Arvo said. "He found some key evidence—a mother-lode of banking records—the end of last week," he said.

"Last week? How do you know so much about this? Already?" she asked incredulous.

"An old friend of mine needed help. So I cut my vacation short by a few days," he said. "Carlson County had been quietly putting together the evidence over the past year. Let's just say that Mendota County put the icing on the cake. It looks like Ruth may be connected to the fraud case, her name turned up on some of the records. But at the moment, there's plenty of other evidence against both her and her son there to keep them occupied for quite some time."

Arvo had corroborated everything Christine learned from the murderer's mother. "What about Ted Nelson?" she asked.

"As far as we know, he isn't involved in the fraud case," Arvo said. Dent told her they located him out on a lake, fishing for bluegills. "Nor the geologist's death. In fact, they said he'd been very helpful in trying to locate the guy. They said he'd been genuinely upset by his disappearance. An internal investigation was already underway. Ted didn't know about it. Considering that they already suspected people close to him."

"Ted will have to go in for questioning," Dent said, coming from his squad car after conferring with one of the investigators. "But it's just routine. Going to be tough on him though, considering that it's his live-in and stepson that have been keeping him in the dark all these months. Carlson County knows they now have enough evidence to charge all three—LaBelle, Ruth, and her son—in the death of Adams. They just located the missing computer and report in LaBelle's Industrial Park Sales Office. That is, once they were able to get Meridee away from there."

Christine told both of them what Ruth confessed to her an hour earlier.

"Well," Arvo said. "It was a good thing I had an excuse to stop by. I was on my way to the Carlson County Sheriff's Office with a CD of the files Kieran found. Fortunately they came by here as well, so I don't have to drive all the way up there after all."

Christine took a moment to inspect what remained of the pole barn. All of its contents, except for the tractor, were a smoking, twisted heap. Even the skeletal remains of the building had vaporized in the heat. "I just don't understand," she said. "How could it be possible for Ruth and Joey to hide their role, for so long? Did Ted turn a blind eye?"

"You know how it is, Christine," Arvo said. "Sometimes you can fool the people closest to you, keep secrets from them even better than you can from strangers. Like that amazing crossbow skill you just demonstrated. I didn't see that coming."

She could see a look of gratitude in his eyes.

"It was plenty sexy, too. You'll have to show me how it works," he added.

"You never change, do you?" she said.

"Would you really want me to find you unsexy? I think not. Thanks for saving my life and showing off a new sexy side of yourself. Now that we aren't coworkers, I can say all sorts of inappropriate things to you. Gotta love that," he said.

"Well," she said, "that's true, I guess, what you said about secrets. My dad would have said that the landscape holds onto its secrets too, just like that, but if you look closely, there are always clues. And he would go on about those clues like you wouldn't believe. He was an amateur geologist practically. I only wish I hadn't been such a bored kid when he wanted to talk to me about it.

"I'm sorry I didn't know him better. He seemed like an interesting guy," he said.

Christine found herself tearing up. "Oh. Damn. I just remembered."

"What?" Arvo said. "What else?"

"Oh, no," she said, seeing once again that the pole barn was a total loss. The kittens had been trapped inside. She couldn't bring herself to explain exactly what she had remembered. She just shook her head, the tears freely flowing. She knew Arvo was thinking that she'd been reminded of missing her dad.

"You've had enough for one day," he told her, helping her inside her house, which survived unscathed except for a few bullet holes for the mice to explore. He had her lie down in her bedroom. "Let me get you a glass of water. I'll see the rest of Carlson County law enforcement gets what they need. Then I'll be right back."

She told him to wait. She wanted to tell him something. He sat next to her waiting for her to say what she struggled to say.

"Jesus Christ, Ivory," he said, gathering her into an embrace. "It's going to be okay."

She held herself away from him, her eyes questioning him.

"You got me," he said "I was coming to see you, you had me worried. You sounded like you needed a friend."

He embraced her once more, her arms holding him tighter than he was holding her. Finally she lay exhausted on the bed, sending Arvo for the glass of water he promised her. But when Arvo returned moments later to the bedroom, he wasn't carrying a refreshing glass of water, but two happy kittens purring in his arms.

"Cats? You?" He smiled broadly, shaking his head. "Like I said earlier, Ivory. After all these years, you still manage to surprise me."

"Oh, thank god you found them," Christine said. "I thought they burned in the pole barn. Where were they?"

"Holed up under your kitchen sink. Looks like they were fighting their own battle. Your vermin problem appears to be solved, on all fronts."

24

"So what's next for you, Christine?" Arvo asked a few days later. He'd stayed in the room Lisa Adams wasn't using, bringing Christine dinner, fielding questions from the press, and arranging everything so efficiently that she began to wonder if she was rubbing off on him.

They'd finished cleaning up after dinner and were polishing off a bottle of wine, unwinding on her patio as evening arrived in Lucid.

"Well," she said. "I obviously do have some more work to do here, even though you've taken care of everything so nicely for me the past few days."

"I'm glad you noticed," he said. "Eventually the women in my life find a way to train me. Well, the good ones do." They both knew exactly who he was talking about.

"But I had to leave something to keep you occupied for the next few months—you know what they say about idle hands. Though in your case, I've never seen you idle. Until these past few days."

"Let's say I'm also trying to pick up the good habits of the men in my life." She held back a smile. "Though I'm hard-pressed to find good habits in the men I know."

He topped off her glass of wine. "You haven't had enough yet, obviously. You'll see my better side in another glass. You're staying?" he asked.

"For a while longer, yes. Now that Ted's been completely cleared, I'm going to officially turn the place over to him to manage. Put a more formal agreement in place. Then, well, I have that new job in Nokomis to look forward to."

Her heart fell as she spoke of the new job. For the first time. Up until then, she only felt relief thinking about it. The past few weeks had changed everything. Again.

"I bet you're excited about that. Starting fresh," he said. "Where the problems will be new and exciting and challenging. Right?"

"Sometimes it seems that way," she said. "Sometimes I wonder if it'll be more of the same, you know?"

"I don't know. Maybe a new job is just the thing you need."

"Well, that's what I thought when I came up here," she said. "I thought that coming up here would give me a preview of what it's like to start over."

"Well, you have to admit you didn't have an ideal start," he said.

"That's an understatement, to say the least," she said.

"But you've got a good pest control system now," he said, scratching Precious's ears. "All the bad guys are gone, right, Precious?"

She laughed. "I wish it was that easy. But I think the worst bad guy is the one inside me. Bad habits. I told you what happened when I got up here." She hated admitting her flaws, but it felt good to admit them to a person she trusted. A person who helped her to feel safe saying she wasn't perfect.

"Organized Christine took right over."

"Exactly. The same personality just plugged in when I arrived at the new place. I don't know that a new job is really going to be the big change I hoped it would be."

"I don't know. You haven't really given change much of a chance yet. The new job doesn't start for a few months yet. Maybe you need to give Lucid a little more time. Give yourself a little more time."

"Do you think I can change?" she said. "Be honest."

"I think I've changed," he said.

"Yes," she said. "I would agree with that."

"And I think it's for the better," he said.

She didn't respond right way, trying to keep a poker face.

"Nice positive affirmation there, Ivory." His face went serious.

Oh, my god he'd actually believed me. "Just kidding, really. You've improved," she considered the rumpled detective closely, and knew she needed to tell him the truth. "Though you have a ways to go."

"I'll take that as a positive affirmation. If I can change, then probably anyone can."

They sat quietly watching the sunset, the sky a perfect harmony of orange, crimson, and purple.

"You know," he said at last. "Your old job hasn't been filled yet."

"Oh?" she said.

"You wouldn't know anyone who might be interested? And of course qualified." He looked hopeful. Was he really expecting her to recommend someone else?

"Hm." She thought of the painful end to her career in Mendota County. She had quit. Given up, perhaps more on herself than on Mendota County.

"Is Sharon still there?" she asked.

"Unfortunately, yes. I'm sure she's one person you wouldn't miss."

Her demanding, irritating, administrative assistant had grated on her nerves.

"I'm sure only one of many people you wouldn't miss," he said.

"Yes, there are so many irritating personalities in Mendota," knowing herself to be one of the worst. "But most of them grow on you."

"Well, I'm told whoever replaces you will be able to make staff changes as they see fit, at least within that department."

"I'll be sure to let anyone who's interested know."

"Do that. Be sure to tell those interested parties that applications are due by the end of the month. So they don't have all summer to figure out what they want to do about the future."

Okay. He did miss her. "I'll get them on it," she said. "First thing next week. Until then, I'm going on vacation here. Maybe get the crossbow target out, ride a tractor around, just relax and enjoy the country air."

"I'd say no one deserves it more than you, Christine Ivory."

The End

ACKNOWLEDGMENTS AND SCATTERED NOTES

SHALE OIL IS CHANGING LIFE in the west for good and bad. North Dakota, home to the Bakken Formation, has seen its population boom with the oil. North Dakota is now the nation's second-largest producer of crude, after Texas. While such a vast reserve brings much economic opportunity, there is a huge strain on all areas of North Dakota economy, including the water supply, government, housing, and more.

As far as I am aware, oil has not been found in Western Minnesota.

I learned much about Lake Agassiz from Warren Upham's (1850–1934) study of Lake Agassiz, ("The Glacial Lake Agassiz") which was published in 1895 as Monograph 25 of the U.S. Geological Survey's monograph series.

For a time, I thought of studying geology, but wound up studying literature. Still, as strange as it sounds, I find poetry in Upham's study. But I'm strange like that, so I'll close out my acknowledgements and scattered notes with his words.

The Glacial Lake Agassiz

DURING THE CLOSING PART OF THE LATEST completed division of geologic time a vast lake stretched from the southern end of the Red River Valley north to the Saskatchewan and Nelson rivers. The late date of its existence is known by the position of its shorelines and deltas, which lie upon the glacial drift and have nearly as perfect outlines as those of the present shores of the Manitoba and Laurentian lakes or of the ocean. This ancient lake, several times larger than Superior—indeed, exceeding the aggregate area of the five great lakes tributary to the St. Lawrence—washed the east and west borders of the Red River Valley and the base of the Riding and Duck mountains. Its surface during storms was raised into waves which formed well-defined beach ridges of gravel and sand, and these are found at many successive levels, showing that the area and depth of the lake were gradually diminished. Before these deserted shores and the inclosed lacustrine area were examined in the field work for this report, their character had been observed and was generally attributed to lake action by the immigrant farmers, who in many instances selected the beach ridges as the sites of their dwellings.

Intervals of small vertical amount divide the consecutive beaches, from the highest to the lowest. Through the earlier and probably greater part of the duration of the lake it outflowed southward by the way of Lake Traverse, Browns Valley, Big Stone Lake, and the Minnesota River to the Mississippi. Seventeen shore-lines on the northern portion of the lake area were formed contemporaneously with this southern outlet. Later the lake was further reduced though stages shown by fourteen shore-lines, while it outflowed by successively lower avenues of discharge northeast-ward. Finally it was reduced to lakes Winnipeg, Manitoba, and Winnipegosis, which are the lineal descendants and representatives of Lake Agassiz.

—Warren Upham, "The Glacial Lake Agassiz," 1895

NORMANDALE COMMUNITY COLLEGE
LIBRARY
9700 FRANCE AVENUE SOUTH
BLOOMINGTON, MN 55431-4399